THE SAM HOUSTON STORY

Even at fifteen Sam Houston was 'different'. Rebelling against life on the family farm, he became, in quick succession, military hero, lawyer, district attorney, congressman and, finally, governor of Tennessee. Then, after a humiliating experience with a wife who thought him a barbarian, he resigned the governorship and, in a bout with 'demon rum', acquired the nickname 'The Big Drunk'. His marriage to a Cherokee brought him the title 'The Squaw Man'. Now he had two shameful labels to live down. But live them down he did, to become one of America's greatest heroes, fighting for Texas' independence against Mexican Dictator Santa Anna with the now famous cry 'Remember the Alamo!'

THE SAM HOUSTON STORY

Dean Owen

Curley Publishing, Inc.
South Yarmouth, Ma.

Library of Congress Cataloging-in-Publication Data
Owen, Dean.
The Sam Houston story / Dean Owen.—Large print ed.
p. cm.
"Curley large print."
Originally published: Derby, Conn. : Monarch Books, 1961.
1. Houston, Sam, 1793–1863—Fiction. 2. Texas—History—To
1846—Fiction. 3. Large type books. I. Title.
[PS3565.W53S26 1992]
813'.54—dc20
ISBN 0–7927–1208–0 (hardcover : lg. print)   91–38398
ISBN 0–7927–1207–2 (softcover : lg. print)   CIP

Copyright © 1961 by Dudley Dean McGaughy

Published in Large Print by arrangement with Donald Mac-Campbell, Inc.

Printed in Great Britain

THE SAM HOUSTON STORY

CHAPTER ONE

At first those attracted by the flames on this April night in 1829 thought a business establishment had caught fire and was burning out of control. But those late arrivals saw that the flames came from a huge bonfire, adjacent to the business district of Nashville. Embers shot into the dark sky, winking red eyes against the stars. Already a crowd of jeering men and women surrounded the bonfire in the clearing. Mixed with the odors of burning wood and hay was the pungent smell of frontier whisky. Jugs were passed from hand to hand and a staggering bearded man in buckskins whooped, 'Burn Sam Houston!'

In the shadows of a barn near the clearing stood Sam Houston, alone, embittered. With a beaver hat tipped back on his shaggy chestnut hair, his blue eyes watched the chanting mob around the fire. Once these people had respected him, but now their hatred had been aroused by his political enemies; those who had seized upon tragedy to degrade him.

Those late-comers, attracted by the fire, shouted questions. And the answers came: 'They're burning Sam Houston in effigy!'

'Good! I want to watch!'

Standing a shade under six and a half feet

1

tall, Houston saw an aisle cleared, as two men approached the fire, a straw dummy slung between them. Dangling from the straw neck was a sign in black letters: *'Governor Sam Houston.'*

As the men swung the dummy back and forth between them, the crowd began to chant, 'One—two—*three!*'

At the count of three the dummy was flung to the top of the pyre where it burst into flames. Houston's mighty frame shuddered as a sadistic cry of joy went up from the crowd.

Embittered and bewildered by the sudden turn, in a matter of hours, from affection to hatred by his people, Houston clenched his huge fists and started away. He had seen enough. Why couldn't they leave him alone? he asked himself. Hadn't he suffered enough? He had done the only decent thing possible under the circumstances. Weren't they satisfied with that? Why didn't they understand that his degradation was a personal thing? Couldn't they let it alone?

But as he started away a wash of light from the towering flames touched his rawboned features. A man pointed. 'There he is! There's Houston!' The cry was taken up by the crowd.

Like a wounded bear surrounded by a pack of dogs, he stood his ground. He stiffened his body as they approached, appearing even taller—a giant of a man. The crowd surged

2

toward him like a dark wave. Forgotten now was the flaming dummy on the pyre. Here was real game, not a straw-filled image of this man who had been, next to Andrew Jackson, the most powerful figure in the state.

But the sight of him towering there put caution in them and they halted uncertainly, growing silent as if in awe. However, a dozen or so of those who had been passing the whisky jugs kept up the taunts. Houston recognized them—tavern hangers-on. Only last week he had lifted a cup with some of them. But now their faces were taut with rage and inflamed from the contents of the jug.

Two of them, more reckless than the rest, tried to grab his arms. But a twisting of his heavy shoulders sent them spinning into the crowd. One of them fell, skinning his face. He was helped to his feet, a trickle of blood staining the front of his buckskin shirt.

A toothless crone gathered her dirty skirts about her and came toward Houston, shaking her fist. 'You slandered the name of a good woman—your wife!' she cried.

'I have slandered no one!' Houston's voice cracked out above the roar of the flames, the sounds of the milling, uncertain crowd.

'Then why not have the decency to speak out, Houston?' cried a man.

'What has happened between my wife and

myself is personal!' was Houston's shouted answer.

'You tried to make evil of this woman you married. It was a despicable thing to do!'

'I say horsewhip him!' yelled one of those who had tried to grab Houston's arm.

Then from the crowd came a feeble voice of sanity. 'No matter what he's done, he's the governor and deserves some respect—'

'The *ex*-governor! He's resigned and tucked his tail between his legs like a yellow dog. He's on the run. It took a woman to find him out—that he's only a bag of wind!'

Houston narrowed his eyes at this, and tried mightily to check his mounting rage. 'You've said enough,' Houston warned them, and again tried to leave.

But those who frequented Moore's Tavern now regrouped and began to edge forward again. Firelight flashed across a lifted jug. The man with the skinned face had picked up a length of wood to use as a cudgel.

And Houston gauged their mood. This was going to be sport for these toughs. The crowd was with them. There hadn't been such an occasion since last winter when some of them had drunkenly come upon the Cherokee sleeping in the barn. They had used their rope ends on the Indian. And later when Houston learned of it, he publicly denounced those responsible.

'Houston, we know why your wife left you!'

4

cried the man with the bleeding face. 'You're only half a man.' He pointed his cudgel at the enraged Houston. 'Them Creeks at Horseshoe Bend never shot you in the shoulder, like you claimed. Their bullet went somewheres else!'

Those who had come to see the fun now suddenly grew silent as if realizing this thing could get out of hand. It was one thing to taunt a man for resigning the governorship when his wife left his bed and board and returned to her father's house. It was something else again to vilify him by questioning his manhood. But the rougher element was more vociferous than before. They crowded up. Two prostitutes from Mother Queen's place on the river added to their jeers.

One of them laughed shrilly. 'You're no man, Houston. You're no more virile than that straw dummy on the bonfire!'

A great jeering went up from those in the vanguard. The fire was dying a little, the shadows lengthening now against the barn wall where Houston stood. Stung by their jibes, it was all he could do to keep from wading into the crowd and cracking skulls. But he was determined, if possible, to keep his temper. For he knew that even though he might stand off some of them, the rest, their courage intensified by the contents of tavern jugs, would drag him down.

Again he started away, and the drunk with

5

the cudgel hurled it straight at his head. From a corner of his eye Houston saw the length of wood whipping toward him. He ducked and it knocked off his hat. A wave of laughter rolled toward him.

Straightening up, he glared at them. 'You've gone far enough,' his mighty voice roared. 'I intend taking a steamer this night. If you have good sense you'll let me go about my business.'

Stooping, he picked up his hat and when his long powerful legs started scissoring shadows on the path to the river dock, one of the drunks mistook for cowardice his desire to be shut of them.

'Let's strip him nekkid and see how much of a man he really is!'

'Aye!' was the shout that went up.

Clenching his fists, Houston whirled to face them. He had been a fool to come here, but the flames of the bonfire had attracted him as it had other citizens of Nashville. He knew the fire in some way concerned him, but he'd had no idea just how much he was despised. The knowledge was almost as great a blow as he'd suffered earlier from Eliza.

Those dozen men from the tavern now spread out, crouched down, hands extended, ready to grab him. But they held back, waiting for one of the more reckless to make the first move. And take the first smashing blow from Houston's fists.

From his right Houston caught a movement. A man almost as large as himself angled in suddenly from the barn shadows. It was his friend, the brawling, hard-drinking Mike Reardon. Or maybe former friend, Houston thought. Houston tensed, hoping that Reardon had not turned against him like so many others.

'You watch your front, Sam,' Reardon drawled, his blunt teeth grinning through a tangle of beard. 'I'll keep these lice from climbing your back!'

'I don't want you mixed up in this, Mike. I want no trouble from *them*!' Houston flung the crowd a narrowed look as if willing them to disperse and let well enough alone.

'But it's trouble they want to give you!' Reardon's broad chest seemed to swell under a homespun shirt. Shaking his fist at the crowd, he shouted, 'If Sam wants to resign as governor, it's his business!'

'The hell with you, Reardon!'

'I fought beside him at Horseshoe Bend!' Reardon cried. 'I'll fight at his side now!'

'Two horsewhips needed instead of one!' yelled the man who had flung the cudgel.

'Gentlemen, make it three,' said a slender, pale-haired man who stepped suddenly from the crowd to stand at Houston's left. His narrow, aristocratic features were tense, but there was no fear, only an excitement spawned by danger, shining in the hazel eyes. In a gray beaver hat,

7

his black suit showing too much wear, he was a contrast to Houston, who proudly wore his gaudy, multicolored Indian shirt. A landless aristocrat who shared Houston's contempt for those who cheated the redman, Jesse Summer had one weakness: a liking for other men's wives. Only last winter Houston had saved his life, jarring a pistol in the hand of an irate husband who was aiming it at Jesse Summer's back.

'I owe you a debt, Sam,' Summer said easily now as the crowd looked on, silent for the moment, but still hostile. 'I'm repaying it.'

'Thanks, Jesse,' Houston said, watching the shadowed faces of the men silhouetted by the dying fire. The fact that two men had dared step up to take Houston's part had given the crowd a momentary pause.

But one of them, drunker than the rest, sprang forward. 'Summer!' the man cried. 'You should have taught Houston your wenching tricks. Then maybe he could have held his wife!'

The thin cord of restraint snapped in Houston. Snatching up the man by the arms, he held him overhead. While the man squirmed and squealed like a hog on a meat hook, Houston hurled him into the crowd. Several of the onlookers were knocked down by the man who was pitched into their midst.

This was a signal for a charge. The first two

came in low, trying to grab Houston by the legs. But Houston's oversize fists struck the backs of their heads like hammers. Knocked off balance by the powerful blows, they struck the hard ground on their faces. They did not get up. Two more surged in, one of them tripping over a fallen man. Houston's knuckles shattered the teeth of the other.

To his right Mike Reardon drove the point of a tough shoulder into the chest of one of them, knocking him into a trio trying to come in on the flank. The three men went down hard.

A shouting giant, trying to brain Houston with a whisky jug, was flattened by Jesse Summer's expertly wielded gold-headed cane.

Again the tavern hangers-on tried to rush Houston and his two friends. But broken heads and smashed faces soon discouraged them. Sullenly they watched Houston and Reardon and Summer back down the path toward the dock. Although the crowd muttered threats, no one came after them.

'We'll sail with you, Sam,' Summer said, giving the big man at his side a tight smile. 'I don't think Mike and I will be very welcome in Nashville after tonight.'

'They've no right to take it out on you,' Houston said bitterly.

'But they will,' Reardon put in. He was using the heel of one hand to dab at a cut on his bearded cheek.

The crew of the river packet *Red Rover* was just ready to cast off as Houston and his friends came aboard. Standing at the rail, Houston bitterly watched the lights of Nashville disappear upriver.

Jesse Summer, standing at his side, said, 'Good-by, Nashville. You gave up a lot, Sam.'

Houston said nothing. He had barely enough money to pay for their passage on the New Orleans bound packet. Jesse Summer, as usual, was broke, having gambled away the last of his lands only a month before. Reardon had spent the winter loafing in town.

'What did she do, Sam?' Summer said quietly, watching the tortured face of this big man who had given up the governorship of Tennessee. 'Your wife, I mean. Was it something so terrible that it made you throw away a whole career?'

'I don't want to talk about it, Jesse,' Houston warned. 'I have a great respect for women. I will never consider airing such a situation as exists between my wife and myself. It would only invite obscene interpretations.'

Mike Reardon said, 'At least you owe an explanation to Andy Jackson. He put you in the governor's chair.'

'I've written him,' Houston said. 'I hope to God he'll understand.'

CHAPTER TWO

Houston stood alone in the darkness. He would return to the Cherokees he had known as a boy. There the fire juice traded to the Indians by whisky peddlers and the soft brown limbs of Indian maidens would help him on his way to a self-imposed oblivion. What else was there? He considered his life ruined by the actions of his wife Eliza. In reality, her blows to his pride were to help alter the course of history.

Although Houston had cut all ties with Nashville there was still a later danger to be faced. While Reardon and Summer were below, the captain came to him, his round face agitated. The steamer had tied up at Clarksville, Tennessee, to discharge passengers.

'I suggest you keep out of sight, Mr. Houston,' the captain advised. 'Your wife's brothers and some of their friends are on the dock, waiting for you. They're trying to come aboard.'

Houston clenched his teeth and peered at the landing, where several heavily armed men were arguing with members of the crew.

Drawing a pistol from his belt, Houston handed it to the captain. 'Keep this. I want no blood to be shed on my account.'

'But, Houston, listen. They're in a foul

11

mood. I suggest you go below and stay out of sight until we sail—'

But Houston was already striding across the deck. Below, his wife's brothers and their friends were menacing three members of the crew who were attempting to keep them from boarding the packet. As Houston came down the gangplank, his hard blue gaze swept over the men. There were eight of them in the party, some carrying rifles, others pistols. Their clothing was spattered with mud and he guessed they had ridden overland from Nashville to intercept the *Red Rover* here.

When they saw Houston advancing they stiffened, watching him warily. The crew members, taking one look at the giant Houston, evidently decided they had done their best at the captain's orders. Now they wanted no part of a brawl involving a man of Houston's size. They scrambled aboard, leaving Houston alone to face the men from Nashville.

Houston said, 'You wanted to see me?'

The Allen brothers seemed taken aback by his sudden appearance. But the taller of the group, a rawboned man with a heavy mustache, shook his fist.

'We didn't think you'd have the nerve to face up to us,' he said flatly.

'I want no trouble with you,' Houston said, regarding the armed men with a strict and savage attention. 'If you have something to say

12

to me get done with it quickly.'

'Houston, the manner in which you have left Nashville,' said the hot-eyed spokesman, 'has filled the city with a thousand wild rumors. Rumors that you were goaded to madness and exile by having detected our sister in a crime.'

'There was no crime at all on her part.' And Houston thought, *The crime was mine, perhaps, in not understanding her.*

'We demand that you give a written denial of this, or else return with us and prove it.'

Houston felt sickened. He had hoped to slip away into anonymity, pushing the past forever from his mind. But here was all the ugliness facing him again. Would he never escape from it, he asked himself?

While he stood there with the brothers of Eliza Allen and their friends threatening him, he knew he did not have the stomach to fight them. But if they pushed him too far . . .

Behind him the captain and some of the passengers had come to peer apprehensively from the steamer deck. On the dock, roustabouts had paused beside piles of cargo to stare, ready to seek cover at the first gunshot. For tension was thick in the Tennessee air and the armed men glaring at the huge man in the Indian shirt looked angry enough to start shooting at any moment.

Houston waved a large hand at the captain and the passengers on the deck. Thank God the

13

hot-blooded Jesse Summer hadn't come on deck, or Mike Reardon either, for that matter. One wrong gesture, one wrong word here could rake this area with lead and some of those on the deck would undoubtedly be cut down.

But trouble or not, Houston knew he had to make his position clear to these angry-eyed men who tensely gripped their weapons.

'I will neither go back to Nashville,' he told them loudly, 'nor will I write a retraction. In the presence of the captain and these other gentlemen, I request that you go back and publish in the Nashville paper that if any wretch dares to utter a word against the purity of Mrs. Houston, I will return and write the libel in his heart's blood.'

The men just stared at him for a moment, then there was a shuffling of feet.

'Is that understood?' Houston added.

The spokesman for the Allen brothers let the pistol he had been holding sag in his hand. He looked at his brothers. 'That seems to be an honorable statement,' he said.

'There is nothing honorable about Sam Houston,' one of the friends put in heatedly.

'You have my word on the matter,' Houston snapped. 'I will say no more on the subject.'

Turning on his heel, he retraced his steps across the dock. Although the back of the gaudy Indian shirt presented a wide and inviting target, none of those on the dock chose to take advantage of it.

On deck Houston stood with hands clasped behind his back, staring in the direction of Nashville, where his hopes for the future were as charred as the dummy that had been consumed on the bonfire.

Still bewildered by all that had happened, he stood there as the packet moved slowly out into the current. And he said silently to the forested banks slipping away, 'Eliza, why—why—why?'

And as before there was no answer. When a storm came up he braced himself, the deck planks lurching under the broad soles of his boots. He clutched a bottle in his hand. When he drank Jesse Summer and Reardon watched him narrowly. Although Houston had not told them of his meeting with the Allen brothers on the Clarksville dock, they had been filled in by the captain. They had been in their bunks asleep and it was Summer who said, 'Damn it, Sam, why didn't you call us? What are friends for?'

But Houston made no reply. His big hand shook slightly as he lifted the bottle again and drank from it.

'Better leave him be,' Mike Reardon advised, touching Summer on the arm. 'There are things a man's got to worry with by himself.'

'I'm afraid for him,' Jesse Summer said, turning away. 'I've never seen a man gripped by such black despair.'

15

If Houston heard he gave no sign. He watched driftwood caught up in the river currents, saw the smoke of Indian fires from the far bank. Clouds had moved in and a driving rain pelted his uncovered head. Upon emptying the bottle he flung it overboard and watched it bobble for a moment in the storm-churned waters. Slowly it gurgled out of sight.

And he thought perhaps that was his destiny. To feel the waters of the river close about his head, to feel the sharp, cold hand of death dragging him down into that unknown blackness. Where a man could find comfort in oblivion—be able not to think—have his mind emptied. Never again to conjure up a vision of Eliza as she had once stood at the foot of the staircase on her father's arm. The shy, virginal Eliza in the glittering parlor and the small warm fingers on his wrist, his ring worn proudly.

What had happened? Why had life played this foul trick on him? Was this all there was to life? You take a woman and hold her in your arms and know that by her very existence you can do so much in the world—that there is no goal you cannot reach.

Was Jesse Summer's philosophy so right after all? That any woman married or not will squeal delightedly if skillfully wooed by the right man?

Sometimes he hated Jesse for this disgraceful attitude toward women. And yet perhaps in Jesse Summer he saw his own lack. Was it this

16

lack of skill that had doomed his own marriage? Was he after all only a savage, unfit for the company of a gentle woman like Eliza?

Eliza, I loved you! he shouted silently at the wind. Far above, wild geese made a dark pattern across the sky, breaking before a gust of wind. He turned his back to the rail and the rain ran coldly down his neck.

Closing his eyes he was haunted by the memory of his wife. Bitterly he relived that last night of their marriage, when she had finally revealed her true feelings. During their brief marriage he had held her in awe, trying to win her with tenderness.

That last night he'd had no inkling of the disaster that awaited him. He was not so unfeeling as to think theirs was an idyllic marriage, but he thought in time this would change.

He remembered coming into the bedroom for what was to be the last time. Remembered how candlelight touched her as she lay on the bed, so still and pale in her nightdress, staring up at the canopy above the four-poster, hands clenched at her sides. In his eagerness to possess her he started throwing off his clothing as he crossed the wide, shadowed room. His bare feet were soundless on the cotton rug. As he approached he noticed that she had closed her eyes tightly. Her mouth was tense.

'Eliza,' he whispered, but she did not reply.

17

And he realized hopelessly that she was feigning sleep again as she had on so many nights.

But caught up by her beauty, he lay down beside her and stroked her flesh tenderly. Finally, realizing that once again he could not arouse her, he lost himself in his own passion. But suddenly he became aware that her eyes were open, staring with such stark hatred that it shocked him.

Bewildered, he said, 'Perhaps you are not feeling well.'

'I never feel well,' she said stiffly, and turned her head.

'Then you should see a doctor.'

'It is a sickness of the soul, not of the body.'

'Eliza, what has happened? Have I done something—?'

When she made no reply he tried to kiss her, but he could feel her teeth under rigid lips. Drawing back, he said, 'I hoped that in time you would be wifely to me.'

Her body suddenly convulsed and she squirmed across the bed away from him. 'You're a barbarian,' she screamed wildly. 'You're nothing but an Indian!'

'Eliza!'

Her mouth jerked in her hysteria. 'Why don't you wear your blanket and go back to the Cherokees?'

'That was years ago. I am not an Indian, I am—'

Huddled at the edge of the bed, she began to sob. 'You're crude and selfish. All you think of is your own beastly pleasure.'

Slowly he stood up, his strong features betraying a mixture of anger and humiliation. 'I am the same as I was when we met. Why, then, did you marry me?'

The truth burst from her with shattering suddenness. 'I never wanted to marry you. It was my parents. They forced me. I love someone else—' Her hands flew to her mouth and she went white, trembling as if she expected him to strike her.

But there was no thought of retaliation. Inwardly he crumbled as the full impact of her declaration penetrated his consciousness.

Stunned, he turned his back and dressed. Then he went into another part of the house and composed his resignation as governor of Tennessee, stating that 'although shielded by perfect consciousness of undiminished claim to the confidence and support of my fellow citizens, and delicately circumstanced as I am, and by my own misfortunes more than the faults or contrivance of anyone, overwhelmed by sudden calamities, it is certainly due to myself and more respectfully to the world, that I retire from a position which, in the public judgment, I might seem to occupy by questionable authority.'

Now as he stood at the rail of the packet *Red*

Rover he was in such despair that the urge to end what he later termed 'my worthless life' was almost overwhelming. Again he considered leaping overboard, but at that moment an eagle swooped low over his head and then soared aloft, screaming wildly. As Houston stared, the eagle became lost against the sun that was sinking below the forested banks of the river.

So gripped was he by the sudden appearance of the eagle that he took it as a sign that his destiny lay toward the west.

CHAPTER THREE

Despite Houston's acceptance of the appearance of the eagle as a mystic symbol, he was not able for long to ward off a return of his despondency. Summer and Mike Reardon worried about him, but Houston would not listen to their pleas to talk about his problems with Eliza and thus ease the burden on his mind.

They journeyed down the Cumberland, the Mississippi to the mouth of the Arkansas and up that stream to Little Rock.

'Here is where we part company,' Houston announced as they came ashore in the spring mud with mosquitoes swarming about their heads.

'Wherever you go we go,' Jesse Summer said.
'No.' Houston shook his shaggy head.
Blanketed Indians wandered the streets. There
were trappers and rivermen. A red-haired
wench beckoned to the giant Houston from a
second-floor window above a tavern.

'Maybe an hour with that trollop would help
you forget,' Jesse Summer said. Doffing his hat,
Summer grinned up at the powdered face with
the red, red mouth.

Houston shrugged his heavy shoulders and
led the way into the tavern. There he put his
last silver coins on the bar and ordered drinks
for them.

'Don't try to slip out on us, Sam,' Jesse
Summer warned with a taut smile. 'We're going
to stick with you like burs in a mare's tail.'

Reardon said worriedly, 'We don't like that
look in your eye. It's the look of a man who
might try and do himself in.'

'Nonsense,' Houston grinned, and poured
drinks for them. Rubbing the beard he had
allowed to grow, he leaned close to Jesse
Summer. He nodded at the upper floor. 'I think
I'll take your advice. She is a comely wench.
Wait for me.'

'That's the sanest statement you've made yet.
She's got a warm eye. I envy you your
pleasure.' Summer lifted a glass.

Slipping through the press of men at the
plank bar, some of them in gamy buckskin,

21

others in damp wool, Houston moved to the rear door. Turning he stared over the heads of the others, winking back at Summer and Reardon, barely visible through the noisy crowd.

Closing the door against the din, he heard a woman say lazily, 'Ain't often I get one as handsome as you. Come up, come up.'

He peered up a narrow stairway, seeing the red-haired woman lounging in a doorway, smiling.

He said, 'Sorry to disappoint you,' and stepped quickly through another door that led to an alley. With a chill drizzle now stinging his face, he hurried to a corral that he had noticed near the dock. There with the last of his money, and without haggling, he bought a dapple gray and a used saddle.

Ignoring the road used by the whites, Houston took the Indian trail down through the wild Arkansas River Valley. He rode hunched in the saddle, his eyes bitter.

He had gone only a few miles when Cherokee scouts hidden in the forests recognized him, and carried the news of his arrival ahead to the camps.

When Houston finally approached the main camp of the Cherokees he saw a stately old Indian step from the log buildings that comprised his 'wigwam.'

Oo-loo-te-ka held out his wrinkled hands to

the mud-spattered giant. 'My son,' he said in Cherokee, 'eleven winters have passed since we have smoked a pipe together.'

'You are a welcome sight to my eyes.' Houston saw that the old man had grown fat and tired.

'You have become a great chief of the whites, and now your path lies in shadow. You have come home to your people, Co-lo-neh. Here our fires will warm you, Raven, and we will listen to your counsel. For these are times of troubles for your brothers.'

But Houston at the moment was little concerned with the plight of his Cherokee brethren, who had been pushed out of Tennessee by unscrupulous agents and their treaties and now were being harassed again by encroaching whites.

All he wanted was to forget the bitter episode of Nashville. This was easy to do, for the white whisky peddlers were pushing through the forests with their jugs. And in addition to memory-deadening whisky there was the tall Tiana Rogers, whom he remembered from his youth in Tennessee. Her Scottish blood mingled with the Cherokee had made her nearly as tall as Houston. In a camp of beauties she was easily the most outstanding.

'I also welcome you, Co-lo-neh,' she said. Her breasts pushed proudly against the thin shirt of silk and below the fringe of the beaded

23

skirt he could see the long, copper-colored legs.

Houston came to stand before her, making a gesture with his hand held only slightly above his knee. 'You were only this tall when I saw you last.'

In Houston's youth she had been ten years old, but even then her beauty was apparent. She had since married a man named Gentry, but had 'divided the blanket.'

Now she waited expectantly in the entrance to her quarters, a hand on the blanket that covered the doorway. Houston smiled and she lifted the blanket and stepped aside. He entered the log dwelling and there were smiles of satisfaction from the old chiefs. The Raven was truly home again and with the beautiful Tiana as his mate he would be the bridge between red man and white, and this could save the Cherokees as a nation.

Lying beside her in the dim hut, Houston whispered. 'Here is where I belong. The barbarian comes home.'

Her soft arms crossed behind his neck and she drew his mouth down to her full, warm breasts. 'It is the Great Spirit that brought you to me. I will be yours always.'

But even though Tiana's love eased some of his torment, his greatest release came in the liquid fire of the whisky peddler.

He would sit alone in the darkness, the jug between his knees. He would stare into the

24

night and remember his youth.

He thought of the life in Virginia that he could barely remember. Then the long journey by wagon after his father's death, with his mother disdaining all advice not to take her family to the wild Tennessee frontier. But her indomitable spirit, passed on to Sam Houston, leveled all obstacles. They were beset by weather and a sick team and renegade Indians. And once some whites tried to steal their provisions during a storm.

But when they finally settled on the land of their choice, Houston found he had little interest in his one-eighth share of the family holdings. Instead he preferred to read the classics, such as *The Iliad*.

'An eye for fine words,' one of his older brothers said scornfully, 'but no hand for a plow.'

After a period of months when Sam Houston still showed no aptitude for farming, his brothers decided on drastic steps. They got him a job clerking in a store. However, they did not reckon with Houston's rebellious spirit. The tedium of measuring grain and calico for the nearby settlers proved to be too much.

One dark night, a copy of *The Iliad* under his arm, he slipped across the river to the Cherokee camp. Although he was only fifteen, Houston was already a grown man. The Cherokees, probably the most advanced intellectually of all the North American tribes, saw in Houston a kindred spirit. They taught him the language and the hoop game and the Cherokee mythology. And there were maidens, eager and young.

Because of his size and capacity to learn, he caught the interest of Chief Oo-loo-te-ka, who took him as a son. This was a great honor and when he was inducted into the tribe, Houston felt as if he were home at last.

Although Sam Houston had little formal education, he decided on a bold move when his months with the Cherokees drove him heavily into debt. Returning to the village near his mother's farm, he surprised everyone by opening a school, hoping by this means to discharge the debts which lay heavily on his conscience.

Even he was pleasantly surprised at the turn out of parents who brought reluctant pupils to his door. And no one seemed to object to the terms of enrollment. Each pupil was required to pay eight dollars a term, one-third in cash, one-third in corn delivered to the mill, one-third in cotton cloth. This last item was designed for the teacher's personal attire.

Rumors of an impending war with England were reaching the Tennessee frontier, but even though the possibilities of conflict appeared ominous, it seemed that she was finally going to

26

ignore the upstart America's challenge to her sea power.

By this time Houston had discharged his debts and closed the school. To please his family he entered the Academy at Maryville. But even as the dull routine of store clerking had stifled his spirit, so did the session at Maryville. His restless mind failed to grasp mathematics, and he became the despair of the professors.

However, just as he had made up his mind to return to a more exciting life with the Cherokees, President Madison issued a call to arms, because England had at last decided she would no longer ignore America's attempts to become a power at sea in her own right.

The twenty-year-old Houston ignored the advice of his family and friends that he should wait for a commission. Instead he was one of the first to take a silver dollar from the head of a drum, which signified his entry into the army.

However, his service as a private in the Thirty-ninth Regiment of Tennessee Volunteers was uneventful. In recognition of his valor he was made an ensign. During his service he had hoped to see action under the command of his idol, Andrew Jackson. This finally came to pass when some Creek Indians, under young Chief Weatherford, ignoring the advice of older chiefs, went on the warpath. At Fort Mims, Weatherford's braves massacred four hundred men, women and children.

With the whole frontier ablaze with rage at the massacre, Major General Jackson's command finally cornered the Creeks at To-he-pe-ka, or Horseshoe Bend.

But it was not an easy trail that led Jackson to this last stand of the Creek warriors. His own command had been beset by desertions and insubordination. And it was not until Ensign Sam Houston led a platoon of nearly four hundred men to Fort Strother on February 6, 1814, that Jackson took heart. The appearance of Houston and his Regulars was instrumental in helping whip Jackson's command into shape for the coming campaign.

It was on this cold, miserable morning that Sam Houston first experienced the brutality of war. A private in the Tennessee militia named John Woods was just coming off guard duty when Houston rode in.

The private, grumbling under his breath about the long stretch of guard duty, was in the line next to Houston at one of the cook fires. It was sometime later that Houston heard a commotion from one of the tents.

Having just finished his morning meal, Houston hurried down to see what was causing the loud voices and spate of cursing in the early hours of this wet day. Private Woods and some of his companions had been eating in one of the tents and the officer of the day had ordered them to pick up the refuse they had scattered on the ground. All had complied save Woods, who had argued with the officer and then cursed him.

Looking around, the red-faced officer spotted Houston as a Regular, and ordered him to place Woods under arrest. Before Houston could get a hand on Woods, the man snatched up a pistol and leveled it.

'I'll use it on the first man that touches me!' he cried. And in that moment as Houston looked into the enraged eyes, he felt an emptiness, a realization that this might very well be the end of his own military career, his very life.

Just then General Jackson, hands clasped behind his back, came striding up. His bushy hair was damp from the mist that dripped from the trees. His features were stern as if carved from the hickory that had given him his nickname. Plagued by weeks of insubordination and mutiny of his rag-tag troops, Jackson was furious when he saw a private standing off the officer of the day with a loaded pistol.

'Shoot him!' Jackson cried angrily to his troops, gesturing at the enraged Private Woods.

Momentarily distracted by the sudden appearance of the general, Woods looked away. And in that moment Houston sprang, his weight pinning Woods to the tent floor. The pistol, jarred from Woods' hand by the impact, sent a ball tearing through the roof of the tent.

'You fool,' Houston said through his teeth as he subdued the youth. 'You'll get drummed out of the army for this—'

'It's what I want!' Woods screamed. 'I'm sick to my stomach at taking orders.'

And a good portion of the onlookers seemed to be silently voicing his sentiments concerning army life.

In irons, Woods was led away, and the camp was of the opinion that the private would get a dressing down and sent home. They weren't quite prepared for the extremes that were sometimes necessary to keep a frontier army from falling apart like rotted driftwood along the river.

Within a few hours a trembling Woods was brought before a military tribunal and promptly found guilty. The sentence pronounced by the tribunal was death before a firing squad. News of the verdict swept through the camp and many of the troopers who had been harassing their officers and more or less leading their own lives as the mood struck them now looked sober and a little frightened.

Even then Houston didn't think the sentence would be carried out. A tormented Jackson determined otherwise. Two days later a white-faced Woods was led before a detachment of Regulars. Jackson, instead of staying the execution, rode out of camp so he wouldn't have to hear the firing.

A volley from smooth-bore .70-caliber rifles ended the life of Private Woods.

When a grim-faced Andrew Jackson returned to camp, Houston heard him say, 'Without an army we'll be at the mercy of the British and any redmen they choose to stir up. This time it's the Creeks. Better the life of one private than another Fort Mims massacre.'

Although the severity of the sentence had seemed brutal, Houston was the first to realize that somewhere a line had to be drawn in the matter of discipline. Already British and Spanish agents were supplying arms to the Creeks. The shooting of Private Woods miraculously ended all thought of insubordination and desertion. And the troops found drilling to be much less of a chore than before.

Two days later they were marching after Chief Weatherford and his Creeks. Weatherford, believing he could outfight Jackson's frontier army, decided to make a stand at To-he-pe-ka, where the Tallapoosa River curved in a broad sweep south of Fort Strother.

For ten days Jackson had led his men on forced marches through the wilderness. They sometimes sank in hip-deep mud, and a few drowned crossing swollen creeks. Houston with his great strength would throw an arm about a faltering militiaman, or give a boost to an

31

exhausted soldier trying to ascent a mud bank. Rain pelted them and they ate cold food and slept on the wet ground.

And when some of the men began to grumble, it was one of the officers who sharply reminded them of Fort Mims. 'The men and old women and the children the Indians killed quickly. They were the lucky ones. It was the young women who suffered. I was there after it was over. Naked white women lying across the parade ground. We covered them decently before we buried them. So don't grumble about cold food and the rain. Remember those raped women. Could have been your sister or your wife.'

Houston sat with his knees drawn up, the weight of a cold pistol at his belt. They'd finished a meal of spoiled beef and soggy bread. And their blankets were moldy. The story of the eyewitness account of the Fort Mims debacle had sobered them. Weary as they were, had Jackson given the word they would have marched all night if they could have been sure of extracting vengeance from the Creeks.

On March 26, 1814, Jackson reached the bend in the Tallapoosa with two thousand men. Against the bleak sky curled the smoke from countless Creek lodges beyond the great sweep of the river.

In the chilling rain Houston watched Jackson and his aides plan the strategy on a wooded knoll, some distance from the hundred-acre peninsula where Chief Weatherford was going to make his stand.

On three sides the peninsula was protected by the Tallapoosa. The opening on the land side was fortified by a breastworks consisting of three tiers of huge pine logs. Beyond the breastworks gullies and brushy slopes and mounds of earth covered by timber made ideal terrain for the type of fighting the Indians knew best.

Because of his knowledge of the Creek Indians and their habits, Houston was sent by one of Jackson's officers to scout as much of the peninsula as possible. Under cover of darkness Houston laid aside his clothing. Wearing only a breech clout and carrying a knife, he slipped into the chill waters of the Tallapoosa.

In his days with the Cherokees he had learned how to swim strongly and silently. The moon had come out and when he cautiously lifted his head from the water to rest, he could see the dark and forbidding river banks at the edge of the peninsula. Once he let the current carry him so close to the bank that he saw a sentry touched by moonlight above him. He thought of the white women at Fort Mims the officer had spoken about. Taking the knife from his teeth he considered throwing it. Moonlight would flash briefly on the spinning blade and the sentry would have no time to cry a warning before the point was buried in his throat.

But caution overrode Sam Houston's reckless urge to destroy an enemy. In the morning a battle would rage upon this quiet land. What was one dead sentry? Tomorrow the gullies would be choked with Creek dead.

He swam on, his nerves tingling. How much more rewarding was this life of danger and challenge, as contrasted to his days of figuring accounts in the frontier store, measuring calico, trying to run his school for indifferent pupils in order to pay off a debt. No, he was cut out for this. The imminence of battle was a tonic. At home in Tennessee his brothers could grow old with their plows and their frugality. He would live to build in the wilderness. Perhaps even an empire.

CHAPTER FOUR

Now he swam more cautiously for he was nearing the tip of the peninsula. And although he could not see them, he knew sentries were above with their rifles or bows that could send an arrow crashing through the top of a man's skull. Keen eyes of the sentries would sweep the river here where the moonlight was strong, looking for telltale ripples.

At last he found what Jackson had suspected:

canoes, cleverly concealed in the thick brush that grew near the water's edge. Chief Weatherford was leaving nothing to chance. In the event he was overwhelmed by the Jackson army he meant to have a way open for retreat.

It was after midnight when Houston's great form emerged from the river. Dripping water, his long hair plastered to his skull, he came up through the ranks of silent troops to Jackson's tent. There he made his report to Captain Moss, who relayed the word that, true to Jackson's suspicions, Chief Weatherford had hidden war canoes at the tip of the peninsula for possible escape.

Somebody threw a blanket over Houston's shoulders and he tramped to a tent and found brandy that started small fires in his veins.

In the morning Jackson dispatched General Coffee with a detachment across the river. There Coffee was to send his Cherokee allies swimming underwater to untie the Creek canoes and lead them back to the far shore. Once the canoes were secured, General Coffee and his men were to be rowed to the rear of the peninsula fortifications.

The sky was clear and Houston noticed that the good weather seemed to be raising the spirits of the troops. They laughed and checked their powder and told what they would do to the Creeks.

While Coffee and his men marched off,

Jackson and the remainder of the army waited tensely.

The hours passed slowly in anticipation of the rifle shot, General Coffee's signal that he had landed on the peninsula.

Artillerymen wheeled into position the two small cannon Jackson hoped to use on the breastworks.

At last the single rifle shot burst sharply in the distance. Instantly Jackson shouted an order for the cannon to be fired. Twin gouts of smoke appeared from the muzzles and there was the whistle of shot. But even at eighty yards the artillery was no match for the spongy logs. The round shot bounced off harmlessly. A wave of dismay swept the ranks and men who had expected to plunge through the shattered breastworks now stood uncertainly.

A great jeering rose from the Creeks behind the barricade. Impatiently Houston stayed with his detachment of Regulars, awaiting Jackson's next orders. As artillerymen tried to reload the cannon, they were picked off by Creek sharpshooters from behind the breastworks. The Jackson men fell back. Houston could sense a rising panic among the men. The Creek position seemed impregnable. And on the ground by the cannon lay the bodies of four dead artillerymen.

Far to the left Houston could barely make out General Coffee's men swarming up the brushy banks to attack the Creeks from the rear. A burst of rifle fire and the smoke from burning wigwams at the north end of the barricaded peninsula told Houston that Coffee's men were engaged.

He saw Jackson, mounted on a white horse, the brass on his uniform catching the morning light. 'We've got to help Coffee or he'll be overrun!' Jackson pointed his sword at the breastworks that bristled with Creek defenders eighty yards away. 'Charge!' he cried, and the drums beat the long roll that sent the Tennesseans swarming toward the Indian stronghold.

The shouted order had brought Houston's long legs to life. As he started to run, a burst of firing from the breastworks raked the clearing. Carrying a rifle in one large hand, Houston sprinted toward the tier of logs. He was forced to leap over the bodies of the artillerymen killed by the Creeks. As he ran a man to his left suddenly faltered and clutched at the shaft of an arrow embedded in his chest. As the soldier went down, the great shouting phalanx of troops swarmed over him like a wave.

Rifles were crackling from the breastworks. As he ran Houston could see the puffs of smoke and hear the deadly scream of bullets.

Behind him a man cried in a strangled voice, 'I'm hit! I'm hit!'

With a surprising burst of speed, Houston

raced ahead of the others, almost the first to reach the breastworks. Behind him echoed the screams of the wild Tennessee boys, eager to avenge, as was he, those who had died in the massacre at Fort Mims.

Slightly to Houston's right, as he clambered up the breastworks, was Major Lemuel P. Montgomery. The major turned to shout something to his men, then fell back dead into the mass of troops swirling to the breastworks below.

Exposed now on the breastworks, Houston knew his only chance was to carry the fight. Three Creeks were scrambling up the tier of logs, shouting among themselves that they wished to take him prisoner. He was a giant among men and would be a prize to torture when the victory was theirs. The squaws would have great pleasure with their knives.

But Houston fired his rifle into the face of the lead Creek. Then reversing the weapon, he used it as a club, smashing his way through the advancing Indians. In a few hectic, action-filled moments the stock of the rifle was as shattered as the skulls he had crushed in his wild advance.

Other Tennesseans were dropping over the breastworks, some of them dying before they could reach the ground. On all sides now the whites and the Creeks were locked in hand-to-hand combat. In the warming air rose the stench of sweat and blood, the shouts of the warriors and the wild yells of Jackson's men swarming over the peninsula.

Throwing away his shattered rifle, Houston drew his sword. When several Creek warriors tried to drag him down, he slashed at them with his blade. They fell back—those who could still walk. As he pursued them into a thicket an arrow struck him in the thigh with such force that he was knocked off his feet.

At first there was only a numbness in his leg, and he was able to get to his feet and hobble about, while he slashed his dripping sword at Creek faces and Creek heads.

He knew that his voice was raised along with the others. But he could not hear his own words because of the din. The numbness of his leg was now replaced by a sharp, engulfing pain.

On all sides of Houston the crash of rifles and pistols was like a continuous roll of thunder. The very ground seemed to shake under his feet. Now and again he would glimpse Andrew Jackson, hatless, waving his sword to urge his men on.

As the Creeks fell back before the furious onslaught, four of them cornered the weaving, pain-racked Houston. Their knives flashed as they closed in. One of them discharged a rifle almost in his face. Houston felt the hot breath of a powder flash on his neck. Aiming for a spongy part of the body, Houston drove his sword blade home with such force that for a moment the Creek brave hung there on the steel, the point of the weapon protruding from his back.

As the Creek fell, Houston lost his sword. Weakened by a loss of blood from the arrow wound, he snatched up the fallen rifle. One of the Creeks climbed his back and lifted a knife. But Houston dropped quickly to his knees, falling forward. The brave was hurled over his head and, with the force of a falling log, slammed into the other two Creeks.

Houston clambered quickly to his feet, but the bad leg gave way and he fell. But by this time his own men were storming up and the Creeks were lost to sight.

In falling, Houston had broken the shaft of the arrow, driving the barb even deeper into his thigh. Desperately he tried to pull it free, but lacked sufficient leverage. The world was spinning before his eyes in a kaleidoscope of copper-colored bodies, bared teeth, screams of a dying militiaman. And everywhere there was the *boom-boom* of the guns, the *whish* of arrows.

On the sun-warmed ground lay the dead and dying. A Creek, trying to pull a knife from his breast, staggered into Houston's view. The brave lurched to the edge of a gully choked with dead comrades. Losing his balance, the warrior toppled in, hands falling away from the knife he had tried to dislodge.

Again Houston tried to pull free the arrow from his thigh, but it had penetrated his flesh at such an awkward angle that he could not get an adequate grip on the broken shaft.

Enraged by the pain, he shouted hoarsely at a passing lieutenant for help. As Houston lay on the ground, the officer grasped the shaft with both hands, a foot braced against the thigh. He gave a hard pull that caused Houston to almost faint from the pain. But the arrow did not move.

Sweating, the lieutenant shook his head. 'You'll have to get the surgeon to remove this!' The harassed lieutenant started away, but Houston grabbed him by the arm.

'Pull it out!' he cried. 'Or so help me, I'll break your skull!'

The young lieutenant went white at the threat of this giant with the fever-bright eyes. But he did as he was told. Wiping the palms of his sweating hands on his trousers, he again exerted all his strength.

This time the barbed arrowhead came free, bringing with it a great gout of flesh.

'You'll do no more fighting today,' the lieutenant prophesied.

'The hell you say!' Houston cried, and went weaving into the smoky haze that rose toward the soft blue sky.

A glittering sword lay beside a dead hand. Houston snatched up the blade, nearly losing his balance. The sun beat warmly at the top of his head. This was not a day for pain and dying. It was a day for a girl along a river bank, and a hamper of cold beef and bread and perhaps a bottle. And when the bottle was empty you would find her soft body next to yours ... Houston stopped, looked around at the heaps of dead. Fever coiled in him and he knew it was madness to consider the warm flesh of a woman at such a time.

Finally his legs gave way and he sank to his knees. Staggering to his feet, he stumbled back toward the breastworks. Everywhere lay dead Creeks. He saw a Tennessee boy with half his face blown off. A horse with a shattered leg lay dead in a gully.

Blind with pain, Houston pulled himself up over the breastworks. At last in a surgeon's tent he received attention.

A balding, red-faced surgeon took one look at Houston's wound and said, 'That leg may have to come off.'

'I'll leave this battlefield whole,' Houston said through his teeth, 'or I won't leave it at all!' After the wound had been plugged, General Jackson, his eyes sick at sight of the carnage he had witnessed this day, came to Houston in the surgeon's tent.

'You're the one who led the charge on the breastworks,' Jackson said. 'Your size was unmistakable, as was your courage.'

Houston's teeth were clenched to ease the pain, but he did manage to give the general a grin.

'You're to go to the rear,' Jackson said, 'and take no further part in the fighting today. Is that understood?'

Houston closed his eyes and perhaps Jackson thought he had fainted. Hardly had the general turned his back than Houston had snatched up his sword and was hobbling again towards the breastworks.

From his tent the surgeon cried, 'You can't go back there!'

Houston did not reply. And as time dragged on he lost track of the hours the battle had raged. It had started in the morning. And from the position of the sun in the clear sky, it was well past midday.

By now the Creeks had broken up in small parties under the avalanche of enraged Tennesseans. There were more than a score of individual battles going on in gullies and on wooded knolls. Houston saw some of the Creeks in desperation leap into the Tallapoosa to swim to safety. But they were picked off by General Coffee's men at the tip of the peninsula.

43

CHAPTER FIVE

At last in the thick of the fighting General Jackson saw Sam Houston, but gave no indication that the latter had disobeyed orders to go to the rear.

'I hate this continued slaughter,' Jackson said grimly. 'Not more than two hundred Creeks left out of a thousand.'

Houston and the other battle-weary Regulars the general was addressing knew what was on the leader's mind. Those Creeks left alive had taken refuge in a ravine, roofed over with heavy logs.

'I'll lose good men if I try and dislodge those red devils,' Jackson sighed. 'I'm hoping they'll surrender. I've dispatched an envoy to discuss terms.'

As the men waited impatiently, a cloud passing directly before the sun was taken as an omen by the Creek medicine men.

'This is a sign from the Great Spirit!' one of them screamed from the ravine. 'The whites will be vanquished.'

Yelling defiantly, the Creeks unleashed a fusillade that raked the Tennessee positions.

Jackson's mouth went white as more of his troops began to fall. 'I hesitate to give a direct order for a charge. Instead I ask for volunteers.'

Hardly had Jackson spoken when the wounded Houston limped forward. His act put new fire in the grimy, tired troops. At least twenty stepped into line with Houston.

His face was smeared from powder smoke. A bulky bandage around the wound at his thigh hampered his movements. 'You know what we've got to do, boys,' he said quietly.

Without waiting for a reply, he found strength to move at a hobbling gait toward the roofed-over ravine. Shouting, the Regulars followed him.

Under their withering fire the Creeks fell back. But as Houston, the first to put his boots on the log roof of the ravine, ran his blade through a Creek chief, he was hit. Two balls of lead struck him in the right shoulder.

'Take 'em, boys!' he cried as he went down.

For an hour he lay unnoticed under piles of dead. Not until the last Creek was killed did searchers find him.

'He's still alive, by God,' one of the men said, putting an ear to Houston's chest.

'It's impossible for him to still live,' the red-faced surgeon said in disbelief.

Jackson, his uniform torn, spattered from the blood of Creek warriors, looked down at Houston. Houston lay on his back, eyes closed. The right arm and shoulder were badly torn.

'I have a feeling this man Houston has a mission on earth,' Jackson said solemnly. 'What

45

it is I don't know yet.'

In the surgeon's tent one ball was extracted from Houston's shoulder.

'No use probing for the other,' the surgeon muttered to his medical aide. 'It'll be needless torture because he can't possibly live past morning.'

But the surgeon failed to take into account Houston's indomitable will. 'I'm not ready to die,' he announced.

On a litter he was taken to Fort Williams, where he again confounded the doctors. Two months after the battle he was finally home, so emaciated his mother hardly recognized him.

While Houston recuperated one of his brothers said, 'You should have stayed to help us work the farm. Fine thanks you get for the fighting you did, Sam.'

'I have my thanks,' Houston said in a weak voice. 'Fort Mims is avenged.'

'Your friends are still celebrating in Alabama,' the brother pointed out. 'While you lie here on your back, too weak to move. And your great idol, Old Hickory, was appointed a major general in the regular army and you get nothing.'

'Jackson deserves it. He's a great leader.' Houston stirred to an elbow. His face was gaunt, his cheekbones prominent. 'I'm going to Knoxville. I need better doctors.'

'Move now and you'll die,' his mother wailed.

But Houston was adamant. After examining him, a Knoxville surgeon said, 'I'm sorry to say that your death is only a matter of days.'

Again Houston refused to die. During his convalescence he kept track of the war then raging between the United States and Great Britain. For a time it seemed that Britain, with her superior resources, would be victorious. A pall of fear descended over the land. But then the tide began to turn, with United States victories at sea, starting with the capture of the British frigate *Guerriere* by the *Constitution*.

Anxious for his wounds to heal so he could get into the fighting, Houston recovered sufficiently by midsummer for a trip to Washington. But the journey brought him no joy.

Even though the United States forces continued to win victories, the British Fleet had slipped into Chesapeake Bay. At Bladensburg, a hastily summoned American militia was defeated. The British entered Washington and sacked the government buildings, then departed.

Houston gathered with other stunned citizens of the new republic to see what the might of Britain had accomplished. Wisps of smoke still rose from the charred ruins of the capitol they had put to the torch.

47

Sickened, Houston turned back to Virginia, spending the early winter months with relatives and friends. At the first of the new year he hoped to join Jackson at New Orleans.

But a man's shout told him he was too late: 'The war's over. Jackson's whipped the British!'

At a time when a lot of the Regulars were being discharged from the service, Houston was promoted to first lieutenant because of his gallantry at Horseshoe Bend.

'I'm assigned to the first regiment on duty in New Orleans,' he wrote his mother. But while in that city he was forced to undergo further surgery for his wounds.

'You'll never be a whole man again,' a gray-mustached doctor told him. 'A strenuous life will never be for you. Better go back to teaching school.'

'I'll live to prove you wrong, Doctor.'

But recuperation was long and tedious. He found himself in Nashville, assigned to the office of the Adjutant General. It was there that he trapped some slave smugglers, but in bringing them to justice stepped on the toes of men in high places.

'You will hereafter confine yourself to matters more in keeping with your position,' said the letter of censure he received from the army.

'I abhor slavery!' Houston stormed. 'I loathe the men who profit from it.' Angered at the censure, he resigned his army commission May 18, 1818.

The act moved him toward the field of politics because in practicing law in the town of Lebanon near Nashville he was elected district attorney. It was then that Andrew Jackson paid him a visit.

'I believe you would be as heroic in Congress as you were at Horseshoe Bend. Sam, I want you to run for that office.'

With his own ability, his genius for oratory, and sponsored by Jackson, one of the most powerful men in the country, he easily won the post. Later, Houston gave up a certain third term to defer again to the wishes of Andrew Jackson, who needed 'a strong hand at home in Tennessee.'

Houston ran for governor of that state and won easily. The night the ballots were counted he appeared in a tall, bell-crowned, black beaver hat and an Indian hunting shirt, fastened at the waist by a huge red sash.

'A half-breed for governor of Tennessee,' his political enemies sneered behind his back.

'My blood is white, but my heart is Cherokee,' Houston retorted. However, his love for the flamboyant, his open defense of the redman helped to ruin his marriage. For in 1829 he married the young and beautiful Eliza Allen.

Although Houston was much older, the girl seemed at first to be overwhelmed by the almost

49

legendary tales of his exploits at Horseshoe Bend.

But then had come the night when she flatly told him that she did not love him, that she had always loved someone else. In fact, she looked upon him as a barbarian. Shocked by her revelation he had decided the only decent thing to do was resign as governor, for how could his constituents have any faith in a man who was despised by his own wife?

* * *

These were the things that went through Sam Houston's mind when he sat on the cold camp ground with the jug between his knees. And Tiana would come to him when he was too drunk to move and help him into their quarters.

Behind his back the Cherokee braves called him 'Big Drunk.' But if a white man reviled him, they would defend the Raven. For he was one of them even if his spirit was drowned in the juice of fire.

The squaws considered Tiana a fool. 'You have taken this man as your husband,' they told her. 'But he is no warrior. He should plant corn and do other woman's work and sit at a respectful distance while the braves tell of their deeds of battle.'

The old chief Oo-loo-te-ka would shake his gray head and the worry lines would deepen in

50

the parchment of his face. 'My son,' he often said to Houston, 'your brothers need your counsel. Let Tiana brew the tea of strength and you will throw off this white man's drink and your spirit will again be young and strong. And you will guide us with your wisdom.'

But when the jug was empty Houston would drunkenly sit the saddle of his dapple gray horse and ride to Fort Gibson.

There at Bowheen's Tavern he would stand at the plank bar. Bowheen was a one-eyed man who sold guns and whisky to the Indians and had on occasion been suspected of stealing Indian girls who were 'pleasing of face and form to lie in a gentleman's bed.'

Bowheen had a fourteen-year-old son named Rufe, who was nearly as tall as Houston. One time when Houston got drunk the elder Bowheen, winking at the soldiers and trappers who came to his tavern to drink, said, 'Show us how you fought the Creeks at Horseshoe Bend.'

'It is nothing for a man to boast of,' Houston said thickly. 'A lot of my good friends died that day.'

'Rufe,' the one-eyed Bowheen said to his son, 'let's pretend you're a Creek. Now you step lively 'cause this hero of Horseshoe Bend is a mighty dangerous fella and he don't like Creeks for nothin'.'

The men laughed, their eyes bright from Bowheen's foul whisky, and the prospects of a fight. And to see the giant Houston blindly trying to stave off the rushes of the youthful, sober Rufe Bowheen was enough to make a man split the back of his britches from laughing.

Houston stood his ground, the image of the leering young Bowheen almost lost in the fog of whisky, the smoke of pipes that swirled about the low-ceilinged place.

Houston tasted blood from the smashing hard young fists. He lashed out, but Bowheen danced away, encouraged by the shouts of his father and the others.

But finally even the soldiers tired of this play and they grew silent and one of them said, 'You'd better stay away from him, Bowheen. If he ever hits you it'll be the last thing you ever feel.'

Rufe Bowheen laughed shrilly and struck at the older man's face again and again. At last Houston was battered to the door and through it. He collapsed in a puddle of mud where the wagon road came down from Fort Gibson itself.

And when Rufe Bowheen started to kick the prostrate Houston in the head, the elder Bowheen got him by an arm. 'Don't kill him. I want him to live. He's so goddamn high and mighty. A man tries to smuggle a few blacks and this Houston yells so loud into the wind that they hear it clear in Washington.'

Houston had staggered to his knees. He glared up at the one-eyed Bowheen, his face dripping mud and water. 'So you were one of them,' Houston spat. 'Slave smuggler!'

'A man has a right to sell horses. He's got a right to sell slaves.'

Houston got to his feet, weaving, his clothing filthy. 'If I had a gun I'd kill you.'

'But you haven't a gun. You have nothing but your hands. And they tremble from whisky. They're the hands of an old, old man. Houston, go back to your Cherokees. Don't come back. Only white men drink under my roof!'

The soldiers and the trappers stared with pity and contempt at this derelict.

Young Rufe Bowheen said, 'Here comes your squaw, Houston.' And all eyes turned as the regal Tiana slipped from her horse and came to stand at Houston's side.

'Come,' she said calmly, 'it is late and you must sleep.'

Rufe Bowheen laughed shrilly, this time at Tiana. With the flat of his hand he felt the front of the beaded buckskin dress. 'I got me a string of beads and a jug of whisky. All yours if you warm my blanket—'

His hand swept down the front of the garment, lay against a copper-colored leg. Tiana's dark eyes looked at the grinning face with contempt.

Houston's hand also moved. It smashed across Rufe Bowheen's face with tremendous force, crushing the nose. With his feet flying out from under him, Bowheen fell unconscious into the mud that still bore the imprint of Houston's body.

'You've killed my boy!' shouted the one-eyed Bowheen, and made a move toward a pistol at his belt.

Houston's mud-smeared face was white. 'I hope so. He's not fit to live. He's an animal!'

One of the soldiers, looking down at the bloodied face of Rufe Bowheen, said to the father, 'He deserved it. Don't push this thing.'

Houston lurched to his horse and rode away with Tiana.

'What have I done to you?' he said miserably. 'How far have I fallen to let a man put his hand on you?'

'That is not important,' she said, staring straight ahead into the woods that were shot with sunlight and shadow. 'The fact that you are shamed is important. Perhaps it is an awakening.'

'I remember my father telling of a soldier who was blinded at Concord. And later this man was kicked in the head by a horse and regained his sight. I have been blind and now I have regained my sight.'

Tiana reached over and clasped his hand. The stoic Indian side of her gave way to the blood of the Scots. She wept quietly.

'You were degraded today,' he said. Then adding, speaking of himself in the third person, in the Indian fashion, 'Houston has allowed his brothers also to be degraded. Houston has been a coward. I believe he has returned to the world of decent men.'

With a joyful cry Tiana slipped from her horse and looked up at him, her eyes shining. 'You are my husband and you have come home again.' She pointed at the river shimmering through the trees. 'We will bathe and then you will prove that you are my husband.'

'You should loathe me for the things I've done.'

Her brown fingers quickly threw off the beaded dress and she stood tall and proud and beautiful with her black hair hanging over her naked shoulders and breasts. 'We will live always in the forests. You are no longer white.'

And when he ran with her into the river, he proved himself, finding in the sweet mystery of her body a new strength and force, a joy both profound and heart-warming. But there was still in his mind a spot of light that was the accusing eye of Eliza Allen. *Barbarian!* her voice screamed at him.

When Oo-loo-te-ka heard of Houston's regeneration, he said, 'It is the ways of the Great Spirit. In this man Bowheen he put the curse of evil so that it would show you, his son, the true path.'

'We will break all the jugs in camp,' Tiana announced.

'All but one,' Houston put in quickly. 'One jug I will save.' He slipped an arm around Tiana's slim waist. 'It will be medicine and soon my hands will no longer shake.'

When a whisky peddler came by to trade, Houston refused to do business with him.

'Young Bowheen has a broken face,' the peddler said. 'He'll never look the same. If I was you I'd quit the country, Houston.'

'The Cherokees have special medicine for a man who insults their women. A broken face may be better than lighted splinters under the skin. Tell him that for me.'

'I will,' the peddler said. 'I will.'

It was the realization that he had reached the nadir of his degradation that caused Houston to resolve that he would come all the way back. It was news of the illness of his mother in Tennessee that helped make his resolution even stronger.

'You come home with me,' he told Tiana.

'It makes my heart sing that you have found yourself. But I will not leave this camp.'

'My wife has divorced me. So don't pay heed to what gossips may say.'

'Sam, I am an Indian. I will always be red, not white.'

'I'll come back for you.'

But she said nothing, standing before the log hut that she had shared for so many months with the Raven. And as he rode out in his

56

fringed buckskins, mounted on the dapple gray horse, her gaze grew misty with a knowing sadness and she turned and walked into the forest.

CHAPTER SIX

Pushing himself and his mount, he at last reached home. Splattered with mud, his hair tangled from the wild ride, he saw his mother for the last time. The indomitable will that she had passed on to her son Sam had kept her alive until this, her favorite, her rebellious son could be at her bedside.

The following month Sam Houston returned to the Cherokees.

'Tiana!' he shouted, but she opened the door of the hut and stood stiffly, her hands at her sides.

And seeing the impassive features sent an old familiar terror through him. 'You've grown tired of me in my absence,' he said, thinking of the night when Eliza had bared her soul. 'You love another.'

'No. But while you were gone I listened to the scream of the eagle. And I looked into the fire and read many things.'

'Superstition,' he said, but his voice held no

scorn. For Sam Houston also believed in omens.

'Whenever you wish me I will always be here waiting for you,' Tiana said solemnly. 'Waiting in the camp of my people, not in the lodge of the whites.'

'What else did you read in the flames?'

'You will become a great man. But your soul will be troubled. You will never know peace. But a hundred years from now men will sing your name.'

Taking her by the hand he led her to the pile of blankets that served as a bed. 'I am tired and hungry. But most of all I need you.'

The beaded dress of soft deerskin was quickly dropped from her strong firmly fleshed woman's body. Eagerly she drew him close, offering herself to the will of his hands and lips.

*　　*　　*

During the long trip to Tennessee, plans of empire had been forming in the back of Houston's mind. Those months when he had been drunk the things Oo-loo-te-ka said to him made only a faint impression. But now he recalled them, and these plans began to burgeon in his own consciousness.

Oo-loo-te-ka's dream was a confederation of Indian tribes, which by weight of numbers would force the acknowledgment of certain treaties with the white man.

58

'They will listen to me in the wigwam of the great chief in Washington,' Houston told Oo-loo-te-ka. 'I will smoke a pipe and say that my brothers are being cheated by the agents of this government of mine that should protect them.'

It was in January, 1832, that Houston and a delegation of Cherokees arrived in Washington and were put up at Brown's Indian Queen Hotel on Pennsylvania Avenue.

Washington was not the same as Houston remembered it from his Congressional days. Even though he had reformed, his enemies kept his past alive. Gentlemen in beaver hats spoke behind their hands when Houston entered the bar of the Washington House.

'Even those rascals the Cherokees called him the "Big Drunk,"' one of them said. A group of women in silks, sitting in the lobby of the Washington House, stared through the door of the barroom at his commanding figure and murmured over the tops of their fans. 'He's a squaw man.'

'He probably has a score of redskin bastard children scampering about the forest.'

'Only the basest of emotions could lead a white man to mix his blood with that of an Indian.'

Dolly Burdette, who at forty had given up corsets and proclaimed her love for chocolate, regarded the last speaker in this foyer of the

59

Washington House:

'Rulinda,' she told the woman scornfully, 'I wouldn't be so hasty in my judgment of this so-called mixing of blood. If I'm not mistaken your grandfather was part Iroquois.'

'That was different—it was years ago—'

Dolly Burdette's shrill laughter echoed across the foyer. Moving to the door where Sam Houston stood talking to a Washington editor, she said, 'Mr. Houston, I just struck a blow for the amalgamation of the races.'

Houston, tipping his hat, gave the mountainous woman a puzzled frown. He glanced across the foyer where she had been sitting with three other women. The face of one of the group was a violent shade of red.

Another reason for highlighting Houston's shortcomings was the fact that he was a friend of Jackson's. And Jackson's enemies comprised a considerable segment of capitol society. Also, Houston's friendship with the Indians brought him into conflict with those who sought to profit by the plight of the redman.

William Stanbery, member of Congress from Ohio, in criticizing the Administration accused Houston of fraudulently obtaining a contract for rations to be distributed to the Indians.

As a result of the inflammatory remarks made by Stanbery, Washington was buzzing with gossip. And Jackson's enemies waited hopefully on the sidelines.

'We've got Houston on the run,' was their greeting.

'Did you hear the latest?' somebody shouted to a group on the capital steps. 'Houston has challenged Stanbery to a duel.'

'That Indian lover Houston will probably insist on tomahawks at twenty paces.'

'It would be unseemly for a man of Stanbery's stature to duel with a squaw man.'

'Say what you want about Houston. If Stanbery accepts the challenge it will be pistols, not war clubs.'

Stanbery's qualifications as a dead shot were openly discussed.

'There is one thing in our favor, gentlemen,' one of the beaver-hatted anti-Jacksonians said as he studied his glass of sherry against the chandelier in the Lafayette Club. 'There is always the chance that by sheer accident Houston will be cut down.'

'No need to pleasantly contemplate that possibility,' said a breathless new arrival. 'I've just learned that Stanbery has refused the challenge.'

But even though the Congressman refused to meet Houston in a duel he did make no secret of the fact that henceforth he would be armed at all times.

When Houston learned he would receive no satisfaction, he felt dismayed. His enemies wouldn't even give him a chance to disprove their charges. To take some of the steam out of his frustration he would pace his room at the Brown Hotel, slashing at the air with a cane, as big as a man's thumb, that he had whittled from a hickory sapling on the trip north.

Houston in his travels about the city was aware of a growing tide against him. All the old stories were dragged up.

'There was something odd about him resigning as governor.'

'I say the people of Tennessee were fortunate that he so decided.'

'Stanbery pinned the guilt on him. Houston is a scoundrel. Cheating the government to help his Cherokee renegades.'

With his temper climbing dangerously, Houston prowled the streets of Washington, his long body bent forward, heavy shoulders leaning into the wind. He did not know Stanbery by sight, but hoped to have the Congressman pointed out.

On April 13, on a spring evening, Houston was walking along Pennsylvania Avenue with Senator Buckner of Missouri, and Representative Blair of Tennessee. He was heading for Brown's Hotel when Blair happened to mention that Stanbery was approaching.

'At last,' Houston breathed, and tapped the point of his cane hard against the walk.

Realizing he had made a mistake in pointing

out Stanbery, Blair said, 'Gentlemen, if you'll excuse me,' and hurried away into the darkness that shrouded the far side of the avenue.

In the uncertain illumination of sputtering street lamps, Houston wanted to be sure of his man. As he came up, Stanbery, nearly as large a man as Houston, looked up, startled.

'Houston!' Stanbery said through his teeth. 'I wasn't sure of your identity until now.'

As he had that night in Nashville when he had seen the mob burn him in effigy, Houston tried mightily to keep his temper under control.

Stanbery had stepped back. 'I want no trouble with you!'

'It's talk I want, not trouble. Why did you make such an accusation against me?'

'Because it's the truth.'

'You have no proof.'

'I have sufficient proof, Houston.' Stanbery started away, but Houston's towering bulk blocked the walk. Senator Buckner hovered in the background, pleading with Houston to come away with him. But Houston heard nothing.

'Stanbery, I want to show you how wrong your accusations were,' Houston said, trying to keep his voice level. 'In the first place—'

'I have no intention of arguing the matter on a Washington street.'

'I wanted to argue it on the field of honor—'

Stanbery wore a brocaded vest, the lower

63

edge barely covering the ivory grips of a pistol jammed into his belt.

'Let me pass,' Stanbery warned, and tried to step around Houston, but was blocked.

Houston leaned forward on his cane. 'I want a retraction. Not only have you damaged me, but my friend Andrew Jackson.'

'I will retract nothing,' Stanbery said heatedly.

'Sam!' cried Senator Buckner.

Stanbery had wheeled away and was reaching for his pistol. The weapon came free in his hand, and those few onlookers who had gathered now sprinted for safety.

Even though the flint of Stanbery's weapon struck fire, the charge failed to explode. And in that moment, with his chest muscles braced against the anticipated onslaught of lead into his body, Houston leaped. Ripping the gun from Stanbery's hand, he hurled it into the street, frightening a team of horses.

As Stanbery fell back, Houston rapped him severely with the hickory cane. But even though Stanbery was caught in Houston's grip, he managed to twist away. Houston still had not regained the full use of his right arm since Horseshoe Bend.

Again Houston lashed out with the cane. Stanbery, covering up, yelled for help. A crowd, always eager to see a fight, quickly gathered. Among them were ladies in silks and

64

men in polished boots, ruffians from the river, and a group of half-drunk soldiers.

Aroused now, Houston overtook the fleeing Stanbery. With one powerful hand gripping the Congressman's shoulder, he struck him several times with the cane.

Senator Buckner cried, 'Sam, that's enough. You'll go too far!'

But laughing uproariously, the crowd joining in, Houston repeated the punishment.

'I don't think I need a retraction now,' he told the Congressman between bursts of laughter. He began to sober a little. 'I've had my satisfaction.'

Drawing himself up with dignity, the pummeled Stanbery said, 'You will find little satisfaction in your performance!'

And he made good his threat. The next day a note was sent by Stanbery to the speaker of the House, saying he had been 'attacked ... knocked down by a bludgeon and severely bruised' by Samuel Houston, late of Tennessee.

After the accusation was read to the House a resolution was offered for the arrest of Houston.

James K. Polk, the President's strong voice in the House, leaped to his feet and cried, 'The House has no power to place this man under arrest.'

However, the vote was 146 to 45 to arrest Houston.

The following day the galleries were jammed

65

and every member was in his seat when Houston, wrapped in a fur-colored buckskin coat, his hickory cane under one arm, loomed largely as he lumbered down the aisle. At his side was the sergeant at arms.

For his attorney, Houston secured the services of Francis Scott Key. But he gave the writer of *The Star-Spangled Banner* little opportunity to conduct a defense. Houston's oratory thundered through the chamber in his own defense. His claim was that he had acted in self-defense, and the trial lasted a month. At its conclusion the giant from Tennessee was found guilty. His punishment was a mild reprimand by the Speaker of the House.

But Stanbery, not satisfied with the verdict, filed criminal charges. After a lengthy trial a jury convicted Houston of assault and he was fined five hundred dollars.

But an investigation of charges that he was seeking to profit from his association with the Indians brought findings from a committee that Samuel Houston stood 'acquitted . . . from all imputation of fraud.'

Because he was in the public eye during the sensational trial, Houston was once again on his way to a position of power. On all sides the squaw man and the 'Big Drunk' was enthusiastically received.

One of the first to offer his hand was Andrew Jackson. The afternoon he was cleared of charges by the committee Houston walked briskly to the executive mansion.

Jackson, his bushy hair giving him a leonine look, sat behind his desk. 'Sam, you have not disappointed me. You took a long, devious trail and for a time I was worried. But now you are back home.'

'You talk like a Cherokee,' Houston said with a smile.

Jackson's down-curved mouth grew sober. 'I want you to know that the grievances you have listed against the Cherokees will be corrected.'

Later, when Jackson wanted a man to gauge the sentiments of Texans regarding annexation he turned to Houston.

'Sam, I have a job for you.' After explaining, Jackson said, 'There are rumors that Texans are dissatisfied with their lives under Mexican rule. Mexico itself seems to be in a state of almost continual revolution. There is a colonizer in Texas named Austin. Among others, sound out his feelings in the matter.'

'I'll send you a report,' Houston said succinctly.

Jackson put out his hand. 'You stand on the threshold of destiny, Sam.'

When Houston rode south from Washington the scandalmongers were again at work. The news of his commission from Jackson had spread.

'Jackson's sending him to found an empire in

Texas!' was the popular cry.

'Houston's dreams are even more ambitious than Aaron Burr's.'

'Jackson should be impeached for putting so much trust in a man.'

Other wild rumors were to the effect that Jackson had an army waiting somewhere to the south and that Houston would personally lead it into Texas.

'Jackson will risk war with Mexico for a handful of Americans ... Any man who takes up residence in a wilderness such as Texas deserves his fate.'

It was well known that Jackson was willing to pay five million dollars for Texas. New Englanders particularly voiced their disapproval. The annexation of Texas would add another slave state to the Union.

Sam Houston, his long figure splattered with the red mud of El Camino Real, the King's Highway, covered over a thousand miles of Texas Territory. He swam his horse across turbulent rivers, prowled the forests.

At San Antonio de Bexar he took comfort in the sight of the stone and adobe buildings warmed by the sun. Here he found his first good weather. He skirted the Alamo Mission and came to the plaza with its coating of dust. From shaded patios came the strumming of guitars, and as he passed open gates he saw señoritas flashing their fans. Sight of a beautiful woman always lifted his spirits, and he was able for the moment to forget the discomforts and dangers of the trail.

On February 18, 1833, he dispatched a letter to Jackson: 'Having been so far as Bexar in the province of Texas ... I am in possession of some information that ... may be calculated to forward your views, if you should entertain any, touching the acquisition of Texas by the United States.'

Finally he reached San Felipe de Austin on the Brazos River, where a settlement of thirty families had taken up residence. Here Stephen F. Austin had carried on the colonization started by his father Moses Austin.

While waiting for an audience with Austin, who was busy with matters pertaining to dispatches from Mexico City, Houston renewed his acquaintance with Jim Bowie. At his belt Bowie carried a large, oversize dagger with a hilt. He had dubbed it the Bowie knife.

Bowie had an engaging personality. He could make himself acceptable to the old Spanish families or be hailed as a *compadre* by those who frequented the rough trail camps. He was from Georgia, sandy-haired, built to the same gigantic proportions as Houston himself.

Bowie and Houston stood at a tavern bar made of unpainted lumber. There they paid tribute to each other.

'You're already a legend, Jim,' Houston said.

'And so are you. But you're also the great man of mystery.'

Instantly Houston's face tightened and he stared down at the bottle on the bar.

'Mystery as to why I gave up the governorship,' he said in a dead voice. 'That's one phase of my life I won't discuss. Not even with you.'

Bowie took this rebuff good-naturedly enough. 'Friend of yours is carrying one of my knives. Almost got his fingers cut off when he matched blades with a pair of highwaymen on the Natchez Trace. He said he'd do his fighting in the future with one of my blades. The hilt can save a man his fingers.'

'What friend of mine?' Houston asked, staring out the window at the rain. Inside there was the smell of wet leather. Voices hummed.

'Mike Reardon,' Bowie said. 'Asked to be remembered to you if I crossed your trail.'

'Mike's a good man. He was with me at Horseshoe Bend. If we have trouble here I'd like him at my right hand.'

'You think there'll be a fight for Texas?'

Many eyes were now turned on the pair at the bar, whose shoulders stretched worn buckskin. Houston shrugged. 'Fight or not, we've got to be prepared. We can't go off with our guns half-cocked and expect to win Texas.'

'I hear your friend Jackson thinks Texas can be bought into the Union.'

'Five million to Mexico is a fair price,' Houston admitted. 'But the North will never agree to it.'

'I remember hearing you say once that if the Abolitionists up North were as human in their feelings toward the redman as they are to the black, their cause would be strengthened.'

'I still feel it.' Houston's blue eyes turned bitter. 'The slave question will have to be solved, for sure. But so will the Indian problem.'

Houston listened to Bowie tell of his latest exploits, but they were not so grim as the days when he had taken part in duels and fought Indians. Now, with an eye to the future, Bowie had settled down, joined the church. With his new wife, Ursula, he had established a fine residence in Saltillo.

Houston found in Jim Bowie a kindred soul. They were both reckless and adventurous. There were many things to talk about, to laugh about.

'Tomorrow is Christmas,' Bowie reminded Houston.

'I'd forgotten. I don't pay much attention now that my mother is gone. I always tried to send her something or see her on Christmas.'

'I'll be away from my family, so how about eating dinner with me?'

'Glad to,' Houston said, and as he lifted his bottle, said thoughtfully, 'When you saw Mike

Reardon did he by any chance mention Jesse Summer?'

Throwing back his head, Bowie let out a howl of laughter and slapped the edge of the bar with a heavy hand. The blow caused bottles to dance up and down the planking. Men stared at the big sandy-haired man.

'No, Reardon didn't mention him, but he didn't need to,' Bowie said, wiping his eyes. 'Summer fought a duel in New Orleans with a certain Monsieur LeGrand. LeGrand had the choice of weapons and asked for swords. Summer could easily have killed him, but he expertly cut LeGrand's belt so that his pants dropped. It was quite a sight, so I'm told, LeGrand trying to run Summer through and at the same time hold up his trousers.'

'The reason for the duel was a woman, I suppose.'

'LeGrand's wife.'

'I thought so,' Houston ran fingers through his chestnut hair. 'I could use a man of Jesse's talents. He's smart and can fight. But he has this one weakness.'

'Well, one thing you can count on,' Bowie said, laughing again, but not so violently this time. 'He won't die of old age.'

'Some husband will kill him,' Houston said gloomily. 'Or hire it done.'

'I suppose Jesse Summer can't be blamed too

72

much. The women in question always seem willing enough.'

'I know that's his philosophy concerning the matter. That if he didn't accommodate them somebody else would.'

'Fair enough reasoning,' Bowie said. 'But hard to convince a husband who's just learned he's a cuckold.'

Later, Houston managed a brief meeting with Austin. Rumors that England hoped to acquire Texas by trade or purchase were flooding the frontier. Austin looked worried. He was a quiet man, with a sensitive face framed by dark curly hair. He had the eyes of a dreamer. They briefly discussed the reasons for Houston's presence in Texas. Austin was noncommittal.

After sharing Christmas dinner with Bowie, Houston rode with him to Bexar.

'What's this about your coming to take over Texas?' Bowie asked. 'Rumors are flying.'

Houston made no comment.

Later when he went to Nacogdoches, where he had visited earlier, Houston learned he had been unanimously elected a delegate to the convention that had been called for April 1, 1833 at San Felipe.

This was pleasing news because it meant that he was really beginning to live down the part of his life he most wanted to forget.

At the convention, Houston argued for annexation along Jackson's plans. But Austin was dead set against it.

'We are a province of Mexico,' Austin said quietly, placing both hands on a blanket-covered table in the shack where the delegates were meeting. 'We make our deals with Mexico, not with the United States.'

Houston leaped to his feet, his Indian blanket coat making him appear even larger in the small drafty room. 'I have given you Andrew Jackson's terms . . .' And he argued for them.

However, Austin said seriously, when he had finished, 'Mr. Houston, I am a citizen of Mexico—an officer in that republic I have sworn to uphold. It is my firm belief that our future lies not with the United States but with Mexico.'

'If we don't ask for annexation,' a bearded buckskin-clad man put in, 'England will swallow us up.'

'England will not risk war with Mexico!' somebody cried.

Austin held up his hands for silence. Then he said quietly, as he looked around the barren room where men in buckskin and frayed homespun had gathered, 'I will make a proposal to Santa Anna. I believe we can deal with *El Presidente*. He has ousted Bustamente, and has the support of the liberals. From all reports he is a reasonable man.'

'What is your proposal?' Houston asked.

'That we become a separate state. That we have our own government in Texas and not be subject to the authorities at Coahuila, as we are now.'

Houston had taken his seat, a box strong enough to support his weight. But now he leaped to his feet. Austin looked a little startled, as if he expected this large-fisted man to put up an argument.

'I will make a further resolution, gentlemen,' Houston said. 'If this is what the majority wants, I'm satisfied. But I would like one point to be added to your resolution. Do not encroach upon Indian lands.'

'We now hear from the great lover of Cherokees,' one man said sourly.

'I'm proud to be an adopted member of that tribe!'

'There's room to the north and west for redmen,' a bearded delegate from Nacogdoches cut in. 'They don't belong in Texas.'

Houston's eyes turned cold. 'We already have red mud in Texas. Let's not deepen the color by having it mixed with the blood of our settlers.'

'The Indians make war, not us!'

'Untrue!' cried Houston. 'Treat the Indian fairly and you will have no trouble.'

'Any sane man knows the only way to deal with a savage is to ram a gun muzzle down his throat.'

★　　★　　★

In high spirits Austin made ready to leave for Mexico City and his meeting with the new *El Presidente*. Houston, in the crowd to see him off, shook his hand.

'Thanks for swinging over to my side, Houston.'

'You have sound arguments,' Houston admitted. 'Texas is in my blood. It will be my home. Whatever is best for Texas is what I want. What we all want!'

A shout went up from the gathering. Hats were thrown into the air. Somebody fired a gun in exuberance, frightening a team of horses. A woman screamed and grabbed the arm of a small boy, jerking him to safety around the corner of a building.

Austin said, 'I'll be back within a few months.' He waved to the crowd that had gathered to see him depart.

After Austin had gone, a Mexican said, 'Austin has more trust in Santa Anna than I have. I hear he eats opium for breakfast.'

'I believe in giving Austin a chance to do things his way,' Houston said. In the direction Austin had taken, a bank of dark clouds built up suddenly. Houston, considering it an omen, shivered and turned away.

CHAPTER SEVEN

The days of bloodshed were at hand...

Because the Mexican law of 1830 had limited immigration, Nacogdoches, where Houston began the practice of law, had started to boom as a center of smuggling activity. There was an influx to Texas of those who for one reason or another decided that a change of residence and climate might be healthful. Because of this undesirable element now slipping across the border, 'Hell and Texas' became a pungent addition to the frontier vocabulary. When those of dubious reputation disappeared from their usual haunts in various parts of the country, friends would say, 'He's G.T.T.—gone to Texas.'

Now, in 1833, Houston found his law practice growing. One day he was regaling some hunters with stories of his days with the Cherokees. A familiar voice said, 'You should be ashamed of yourself. Giving the slip to a pair of good friends like you did.'

Houston looked around to see Jesse Summer. And at his elbow was a bearded, grinning Mike Reardon.

With a glad cry Houston embraced them both, and with a mighty sweep of his huge arms bore them to a tavern.

'Drinks for everybody!' he shouted. Then he added soberly, as bottles were set out, 'Jesse, I thought you'd be dead by now.'

'Husbands will have to improve their aim.'

Houston laughed, draped a heavy arm across Reardon's thick neck. 'And I thought by this time you'd have your skull broken by a pickax.'

'No pickax made could dent this head of mine.'

Laughing, they took their bottles to a quiet table. Houston let his blue gaze take in Summer's new broadcloth, the shirt of China silk, the boots of soft black leather.

'You seem to have found a new prosperity,' Houston said, his eyes twinkling. 'What was it this time? Spanish dice or a horse race? Or did the father of some married daughter pay you a handsome fee to get out of town before the husband put a bullet between your teeth.'

Summer shrugged. 'I'm a businessman now, Sam. A dealer in French wines.'

'I hope you don't plan to sell French wines in a place like Nacogdoches,' Houston said with a laugh.

Summer's aristocratic features were serious. 'Sam, the frontier is changing. You'd be surprised.'

'Maybe the rest of the frontier, but not Texas.'

'We're in a great era of peace,' Jesse Summer said soberly. 'Santa Anna is a reasonable man. I have friends in New Orleans who know him well. Under his rule Texas can't help but prosper. That's why I'm here. And to see you, of course.' Summer smiled. 'Mike here came to drink up all the whisky in Texas. If there's any left after you're through with it, that is.'

Houston started to smile, then he grew serious. 'I still like my drinks. But not in excess. I tried to run away. You can't do it, Jesse. Life has a habit of catching up with you.'

For the next few weeks Houston was busy with affairs of state that he had assumed as a delegate. Because of Mexican law, requiring that all owners of land must be of the Catholic faith, Houston was converted by Father Muldoon.

He was becoming successful in the practice of law. And even though Austin's meetings with Santa Anna had dragged on and on, most citizens still had hope.

It was at this point that Houston sent word to Tiana, urging her to join him and take her rightful place as his wife. But she declined, reminding him that she would be waiting, but only if he returned as a Cherokee. She would not live among the whites.

One of Houston's clients was the Burke Tweedy—Bricido Barreras Freight Line. Alongside the towering Houston Barreras looked like a plump little dwarf.

Burke Tweedy had a fondness for French

wines, something he could never have afforded before his new-found affluence. Houston had been a guest at Tweedy's wedding the year before and at the reception that lasted for three days. Tweedy, a heavy-gutted, red-necked, quarrelsome man, had married the very young and very beautiful Iris Baintree. There were rumors that her father had been in Burke Tweedy's debt. Houston had heard that the father's obligations to Tweedy were satisfied by this marriage of convenience.

Iris had red hair and was very pale and demure. Because she had spent her girlhood in New Orleans, she found the new importer of French wines, Jesse Summer, to be a lively companion. There was nothing Mrs. Iris Tweedy enjoyed more than Summer's anecdotes concerning New Orleans society.

One day Houston ran into his friend on the street. 'A word of warning, Jess,' Houston said. 'Tweedy's lived long enough in Texas to react to situations like a Mexican.'

'What situations, Sam?' Summer asked blandly.

'Wife-stealing, for instance. This time there'd be no encounter with pistols. But a cutting with a knife where it would be most effective. Do I make myself clear?'

'You've been too long with the Cherokees,' Jesse Summer said, trying to make light of it. 'You may accept their uncivilized ways, but no other white man would do such a thing to another.'

At that moment came a shout as a coach from Mexico City swirled in, raising a great cloud of dust. In the mail pouch was the startling news that Stephen Austin, instead of being treated as an official of the Republic of Mexico, had been thrown into prison by Santa Anna.

'Austin is a sensitive man,' one of the citizens of Nacogdoches cried, when a crowd gathered about the coach. 'He'll suffer greatly.'

No matter what his own predicament might be, Austin, in his cautious way, advised his fellow Texans to bide their time and wait.

In a letter addressed to the people of Texas and read aloud by Houston, Austin said, 'Do not blame the government for arresting me. And I particularly request that there be no excitement about it ... keep quiet ... discountenance all revolutionary measures or men ... Have no more conventions.'

Immediate cries for armed intervention swept through the crowd. Mike Reardon, always eager for a tavern brawl or a full-scale war, shook his fist in the direction of Mexico City.

'I say, let's go down and get Austin out of that Mex prison and bring him home!'

Houston held up his large hands to silence the gathering of angry men. 'We can't afford a war now, boys!'

'Are we going to let them treat Austin like a

common thief?' an onlooker cried.

Another said, 'I hear he's in a dungeon. Without food or water.'

Houston shouted down the clamor that resulted from this statement. 'You'll hear many things before this is over. But listen to me. We can't afford a bloody struggle now. And we'll have one if we try to interfere.'

'Blood has flowed before in Texas!'

'Listen to me, boys!' Houston cried. 'Can't you see that this is what Santa Anna wants?'

'How do you know what Santa Anna wants!'

'What chance would we have against the might of Mexico?' Houston's angry eyes swept the crowd. 'Use your head, you fools!'

But even Jesse Summer, standing straight and slim in the crowd, seemed doubtful. 'Sam, for once I'll have to take a stand against you.'

'I'm all for making a show of strength,' Houston said, trying to remain calm. 'But only when we are prepared. You understand that? *When we are prepared!*'

'When'll that be?' somebody said thinly.

'When we have an army. Not a ragtag pack of citizens trying to stand up against trained soldiers. We need time.'

Some of the crowd were obviously swayed by Houston's oratory. Taking this moment, Houston got Summer by the sleeve of the latter's fine broadcloth coat and drew him aside.

'Help me in this, Jesse,' he urged. 'You have

influence here.' Then he added, 'At least among the ladies. And they in turn can influence their husbands.'

'I don't know, Sam—'

'I've changed my views considerably in the past weeks. Now I favor independence from Mexico.'

'The Republic of Texas,' Summer breathed. 'By God, Sam, you might just be able to put it across.'

'But we need time, as I said. Play into Santa Anna's hands now and we'll all be crushed. Then England or some other European power can step in and use their own bandages to bind up our wounds.'

Summer's eyes began to shine. 'What will independence mean to a businessman such as myself? Will I fare better or worse?'

'You ought to know the answer to that. Santa Anna has shown by his actions that he will never consider us anything but vassals. We'll have our own government. This republic of ours can prosper, don't worry about that.'

'I see, I see.'

'There's a great chance here, Jesse. And not just for a dealer in French wines. You only dabble in that. It isn't business for a man like you. You could come into the government. I tell you, Jesse, before it's over we may all have our names engraved in bronze.'

83

'You've forgotten Andy Jackson. He favors annexation.'

'I can see now that the North will never let us in. They'll fight us all the way to keep us out of the Union.'

'The other night I dreamed that the North and South went to war over the slave question.'

'Men will argue and shout,' Houston said, 'but they'll never go to war over it. Any rational man with a spark of humanity in his breast knows that slavery is doomed. It will be gone and forgotten long before we could get around to fighting over it.'

'I hope you're right, Sam. I surely hope you're right.'

Houston caught a glimpse of a slender red-haired woman, a parasol over her shoulder, strolling through the crowd. Men stepped aside, tipping their hats. Some of them looked at the woman, then at Jesse Summer. Summer pretended not to notice her. But in a moment when she was out of sight, he told Houston that he'd see him later, and strolled in the direction taken by the woman.

Summer hurried to his business establishment, a small storeroom with sleeping quarters in the rear. Despite the one fine suit and the talk of financial success, his role as wine merchant was not very rewarding. Cautiously he keyed open the front door, glancing up and down the street. But no one was paying any attention to him. The town had been rocked by

84

news of Austin's imprisonment.

Shutting the door against the street, he covered the window and then went to the rear. Here he slept and sometimes took his meals when he could not afford to eat at Mrs. Boarding's.

He closed the door. There was another door with a heavy bolt, that opened off the alley. Across the room was a chest of drawers, a small trunk and a straw mattress covered by a serape which served as a bed.

On this sat Iris Tweedy, in a very unlady-like position, the handle of her parasol between her knees.

'I imagine your husband is on another trip,' Summer said coolly, taking in her beauty, the pale skin, with just a trace of the freckles she tried mightily to hide with face powder. Her breasts were of such magnificent proportions that he was always struck with the incongruity of such a slender back being their only support.

'Burke said he had to go and see Barreras,' she said. Barreras, Burke Tweedy's partner, now lived at Saltillo. 'Something about extending the line to Santa Fe.' She looked across the room at Jesse Summer. 'You haven't bothered to greet me properly.'

'You shouldn't have come here in broad daylight.'

'I want and need you.'

85

'I didn't care for you parading in front of that crowd.'

'You're ashamed of me.'

'Hardly,' he said, 'but you do offer somewhat of a show with that bosom of yours.'

She got up off the bed, two spots of color on her cheeks. 'I don't have to come here and be insulted, Jesse.'

'Oh, sit down and be quiet.'

The hazel eyes darkened. 'I'm hardly in a mood to be talked to this way.' She beat the toe of a small foot against the bare floor.

'I'm not interested in your moods.'

'What if I told you it was four times last night with Burke?' she said, watching him. 'Would you be jealous?'

'I have a feeling you brag about your husband's capacity for bedroom warfare. He drinks too much. I doubt if he's up to four excursions to bliss.'

'It was four, maybe five times, for all I remember. Burke says he wants to be sure I won't look at another man while he's gone.'

'If it's true, he doesn't seem to realize that by such tactics he leaves you more vulnerable than ever.'

'Sometimes I wish I'd never met you, Jesse.'

'I'm sorry these conditions at home have upset you again.' For the first time he smiled, and removed his jacket and hung it on a peg. 'You just worry me a little is all. People are beginning to talk about us.'

86

'I don't want to come here to you. But I can't help it. It's a weakness that I despise in myself.'

'Don't despise something that brings so much pleasure.'

'I overheard Burke talking with a man who says that General Santa Anna eats opium. Do you believe that, Jesse?'

Summer shrugged. 'Who knows?'

'I sometimes think I should turn to opium. It should be safer than coming here to you.'

'Am I a narcotic for you?'

'Jesse, are you just going to *stand* there? I'm so-so on edge—'

'Ah, yes, your husband's four blundering nocturnal attempts to prove his masculinity to you.'

'Don't make light of it, Jesse,' she warned. 'Overwrought as I am, I'll leave here and—' She broke off, biting her lips.

'Leave here and what?'

'Give myself to the first man who comes along!'

'That statement hardly becomes you.'

'There's a shack south of town. Oh, I've heard talk of it. Your friend Mike Reardon goes there, so I hear.'

'That sort of gossip is not for your pretty ears.'

Her gaze darkened as she unlaced her shoes. 'You don't go there, do you, Jesse?'

'No.'

'I couldn't stand it if you went with one of those women and then came to me.' Her voice faltered and she fell back on the bed, forearm over her eyes, watching him.

Summer glanced at his reflection in a rectangular broken looking glass he had fastened to the wall. Damn it, he had a few more gray hairs at the temples. And the lines around his eyes ... Well, this little affair with Iris Tweedy could be very damaging to his constitution; most nights she came here because her husband spent his evenings at the tavern. Summer peered again at the mirror. He wasn't any youth and he seldom faced up to it. The fleeting years were a subject that pained him. In the looking glass he saw her long, satin-skinned body against the Mexican serape that covered the bed. She had deftly removed her clothing. The nipples of her magnificent breasts were at attention.

If only she weren't so demanding. Good God, her demands could plow under a less hardy male.

Quickly matching her own nudity he lay down beside her on the bed. The palm of his hand stroked her back and he felt her shudder. Then he bent to caress her breasts with lips and tongue. She squirmed against him, her knees falling apart.

'Jesse,' she moaned and upon receiving him, caught the lope of his ear in her teeth. 'Why do

I get so damnably passionate?'

'A delightful question that needs no answer.'

'Burke gets me this way. He fools and fools and—'

'And what?' he said when she broke off quickly.

'Nothing. Don't pay any attention to what I say, Jesse.'

'Are you hinting that Burke Tweedy has lost his powers?'

'Oh, no, nothing like that,' she whispered to still his quiet laughter. 'Love me, Jesse. Love me.'

There was a rap of knuckles on the alley door. Summer froze, and the wildly undulating form under him was suddenly stilled.

'Jesse,' she said hoarsely as the knock was repeated.

Summer placed a forefinger against her lips. Quietly he disengaged himself and stood up.

The knock again and then Sam Houston booming, 'Jesse, are you in there?'

'I—I'm busy, Sam.'

'Just thought maybe you'd like to come with me to a meeting.'

'No—I have some accounts to go over. But thanks.'

'There will be some prominent people there. Among them Burke Tweedy.'

Jesse Summer held his breath.

Houston continued, 'Tweedy was supposed

to go to Saltillo to see his partner. But he heard about Austin being imprisoned. He returned to town. I understand he's worried because Mrs. Tweedy wasn't home when he got there. Take care, Jesse.'

Houston's voice and heavy step faded down the alley.

'It was Sam's way of warning me,' Summer said.

'Houston knows about us, doesn't he?'

'The only thing to concern you is to get home. And quickly.'

'Not *until*, Jesse.' She lay back. 'First I've got to have this. I don't care if Burke comes here and kills me. I've got to have it.'

Summer's proficiency enabled the job to be swiftly done. And soon she was smoothing her clothing over herself, checking each item to make sure it was properly arranged.

'I looked forward to the weeks Burke would be gone,' she whispered, her eyes bright now. 'But we'll manage. Tonight he'll be drunk again at the tavern. I'll be back.'

Kissing him lightly, she peered out into the alley. In a moment she was gone.

CHAPTER EIGHT

At the meeting the citizens were openly defying Sam Houston, recommending that an army be raised so that Austin could be rescued.

The clamor did not subside for two days. On the third night Iris Tweedy was able to visit again the quarters off the alley. Her husband was at the tavern, drinking, brawling.

'Oh, Jesse,' she whispered, as she slipped into the darkened room. 'There is so much talk of war. You might have to go and be killed and I'd never see you again.'

'The fortunes of war, as they say.'

'You take it light enough,' she accused. 'Don't I mean anything to you?'

'Of course.'

'You've opened up my life for me, Jesse. I—I didn't know of this—this love until you aroused me.'

'You have a husband,' he reminded her.

'There are things about him I could tell you. But if he ever found out he'd do something terrible.'

'He'd probably try and kill you if he found us together.'

'Kill you,' she said. 'But not me. He'd make my life a hell. But he wouldn't destroy me.'

'These things you could tell me about him.

I'm frankly curious.'

She took his hands in hers and drew him to the bed. A subtle, warm scent emanated from her body. 'Jesse, you've got to take me away.'

'You have a position here of some importance. Your husband is well on the way to becoming a rich man.'

She sat up and said angrily, 'You started this with me. I didn't.'

'You wanted to.'

'Not until that day. You had me sample your wines. My head got light. You kissed me. The next thing I knew I was on this bed. No, Jesse, I didn't want it. Not then.'

'Don't overdramatize.'

'Listen to me, Jesse.' Her anger was gone now. 'You're responsible for the way I am. I didn't know what hellfire lay just beneath the surface. You've kindled it, Jesse. I simply can't let you go out of my life. What will happen to me?'

'Surely Burke is good for something.'

'I don't want to discuss him,' she said in a dead voice. 'We could go north. Chicago, perhaps. I could divorce Burke and we could be married.'

'The plan has some merit,' he said, acutely aware that she was on the verge of hysteria.

'Or we could go to New Orleans. We both love it there. It's what brought us together in the first place.'

'Yes,' he agreed. What he had considered an interesting flirtation had turned into something else again. Had he weeks ago even remotely suspected the fires he would unleash in this woman, or what she would do to him, he would never have pursued her.

She crossed the room and lighted a candle and held it high so she could study his face. 'I understand,' she said, her voice calm now. 'I suppose there is an Iris in every town you visit. Married, of course, so that in the event of—shall we say an accident?—you'll have no worries. Because the husband will be overjoyed that at last, or again, his wife is with child.'

'You're twisting the blade of a barbed sword in my heart, Iris. I'm not as much of a cad as you try to make me out. But these are hectic times. I might have to go off to war. This is no time for me to tear you away from a husband who can give you physical comforts—'

'Physical comforts.' She began to laugh and it rose sharply into hysteria. He slapped her across the face, then took her in his arms. They fell across the bed together, their bodies joining in a savage rhythm of violence and sensation. Iris yielded herself to him, guiding his hands to her opulent breasts, her nerves on fire as a deep, driving passion assailed her.

This night he felt a sudden burgeoning love for her and it frightened him. He knew he'd risked enough already with her. To be drawn irrevocably into her net would mean disaster.

Later he said, 'For both our sakes we should terminate this engagement.'

She wept a little, then said shakily, 'I hope it ends as easily as you wish.'

As she put on her clothing he tried to get her to say what she meant by the remark. She refused to talk about it, and left without saying good-by.

For several days he felt a slight uneasiness. But when he did not see her on the street, he felt relieved. In a tavern he got Sam Houston aside.

'Sam, I've truly reformed. You knocking on my door that afternoon sobered me considerably.'

'I'm thankful for that, Jesse. I imagine Burke Tweedy could be ugly under certain conditions.'

During the next few weeks, while Houston exchanged correspondence with Andrew Jackson regarding the Texas situation, and practiced law, Summer was faced with a crisis. Thankfully he had managed to rid himself of the burden of his affair with Iris Tweedy. True, he did miss her, but he knew that as long as the break had been made it was best for all concerned not to re-establish the connection. Although common sense told him he should leave town, he was not forgetting that Houston had suggested he make himself ready to assume a position of some importance in the new government. Who would be more certain to share in the riches of a new land than those close to the government?

However, on this bright day as he was contemplating his dream, the alley door suddenly opened. Iris Tweedy, her face flushed, came in, closed the door and hurriedly bolted it.

Her appearance shocked him. She was pale as death around the mouth and a certain wildness in her eyes made him uneasy. 'I thought we decided it best that we didn't see each other,' he said lamely.

'Someone else has decided that. Call it nature or God or whatever.'

He felt a coldness uncoiling in the pit of his stomach. 'What are you trying to say?'

'I am with child.'

So great was his relief that he wanted to shout. But he held himself in. She had seemed frightened to death, and he had expected the worst—that somehow Burke Tweedy had found out about their affair, even though it had been over for weeks.

With a trembling hand he lifted a handkerchief to his moist forehead. 'I don't see that's any problem,' he said, trying to keep relief from showing in his voice. The minds of women took strange and devious paths at such a time, he knew. 'Your husband will welcome a child.'

'You don't understand.' Her mouth was shaking now. 'He's never touched me. Not once.'

For a moment Jesse Summer was too stunned to realize just what she meant. Then his eyes were shot with anger. 'You're lying.'

'He's never touched me. Not once.'

'You mentioned four times in one night,' he reminded her thinly.

'I said that to try and make you jealous.'

The way she watched him was unsettling. 'But your husband—well, one thing for certain, you were not a virgin when you came to me.'

'Just before I married Burke there was a cavalry officer in New Orleans. That's why my father moved here in the first place. To get me away from him. I—oh, Jesse—' Tears started making irregular patterns across her face.

The enormity of his predicament finally reached him, 'Good God, you mean Burke Tweedy is incapable of performing—' He grasped for words. 'You mean he's unable to—to make love to you?'

'That is exactly what I mean,' she said stiffly.

He began to pace the small room, brushing past the bed where he had found such pleasure. Now the bed was mocking him. 'Why in heaven's name didn't you tell me about Burke?'

'I started to a couple of times.' She dried her

96

eyes. 'But it's not a thing a woman is proud of. Now do you wonder that I received you so passionately?'

He felt as if he were walking across a fire pit on a greased pole. 'Under such circumstances he is not legally your husband. Don't you see—'

'But I'm still with child.'

'Yes, yes.' He bit his lip and tasted blood.

'At first when Burke didn't touch me I was pleased. I never wanted to marry him. I did it to please my father. And then you came along, Jesse. My placid, nunlike life was shattered.'

'It might have been any man,' he said sharply.

'I came to you because I loved you. I'm not a whore!'

'You're a lady,' he snapped. 'Talk like one.'

'Jesse, you must help me. You've got to help me!'

'Let me think, let me think.'

'It's *your* child, Jesse.'

A sense of being pressured caused him to strike back. 'I have no assurance it's my child!'

She looked at him for a long moment. 'What I have told you is a great shock. It is also a great shock to me. I'll give you time to think this over. I think it would be the decent thing for you to take me away.'

'So this is how you hope to trick me into going away with you!'

'This is no trick, Jesse.' Her voice was cold.

'I'll leave you for now. Tomorrow I want an answer.'

When she had gone, Summer sank to the edge of the bed, his head in his hands. 'Of all the incredible situations,' he said aloud. He knew she had trapped him neatly, whether by accident or design. But he knew that if he ever hoped to live with himself again, he would have to do as she asked. It was his responsibility.

After making this decision he felt a little better. His whole life would be changed, but what man wasn't a victim of fate?

*   *   *

Sam Houston had a visitor that afternoon at his office. Burke Tweedy, stocky, balding half-owner of a freight line, stalked to Houston's desk.

'Is this a business call,' Houston demanded without much cordiality in his booming voice, 'or have you come to tell me that with five hundred men we can whip the armies of Mexico?'

'I've come for some advice,' Tweedy said, his eyes cold. There was about his face the loosened-muscle look of the heavy drinker. Houston had heard stories of him—how he found a savage pleasure in beating a man with his fists.

'This is a frontier.' Tweedy's voice was

98

shaking from some inner emotion. 'But we do have laws. Right?'

'We like to think we have laws.' Houston stood up, towering over the other man. Tweedy's belligerence made him cautious. 'Just what laws are you referring to?'

'The one pertaining to murder.'

'I'd say that is one law that is in effect, no doubt about that. Has somebody been murdered?'

'What is the penalty for cold-blooded murder?'

Houston stared thoughtfully, wondering what it was that seemed to be tearing the man apart inside. 'Death by hanging is the penalty. You know that. Just why did you ask?'

Instead of answering, Burke Tweedy walked to the window and stared out at the street. 'It's either mud or dust. Houston, you'll never make anything out of Texas.'

'That remains to be seen.'

'I should never have come here. It's been the downfall of a lot of other good men.'

'You consider yourself a good man, Tweedy?'

'I'm reasonably decent.' Tweedy turned his back to the window. 'I had an injury when I was young. A buggy I was riding in splintered on a sharp rock when the team ran away. I never intended to marry.' His eyes looked sick. 'Then I came here. And over much whisky and good wine and food I was persuaded to forget a sizable amount of money owed me. I thought I could have a toy doll. That I could touch it and walk with it and—I suppose you've guessed by now.'

'Guessed what?' Houston said carefully.

'Guessed—or maybe the word has gotten around already. Your friend Summer—' Tweedy made a cutting motion with a square hand.

'Jesse Summer has been my friend for years. I don't always condone his actions. But he's still my friend.'

Tweedy gave a shaky laugh. 'Due to that injury I told you about, I am incapable of acting the part of a husband. And my wife is with child.'

Houston clenched his large hands into fists, but said nothing.

Tweedy looked him in the eye, the belligerence stirring in him again. 'Houston, are you a man of your word?'

'I am,' Houston said quietly.

'You swear that any man who commits an act of murder in this town is hanged by the neck?'

'Yes, I swear that, but—'

A drop of spittle appeared at a corner of Tweedy's mouth. 'I may find it hard to hold up my head when the story gets out. Men will laugh behind my back. But I think I have sufficient courage to face up to it.'

When Tweedy was gone, Houston clapped on his hat, and angrily strode out of his office. In the crowded street where people spoke his name, he did not turn his head. Hands clasped behind his back, he walked purposefully to an alley.

'I wonder what's happened?' a man said. 'Sam acts as if he heard the British had landed at Galveston Island.'

'Likely he's had news from Austin. When Sam moves like that he's like a treed cat with a thorn in its foot. Best to keep away from him.'

Houston knocked on Jesse Summer's door, but received no answer. Then he began a tour of the taverns. Finally in one of them he found Mike Reardon slumped across a table. Catching Reardon by his thick black hair, Houston jerked him to his feet.

'You damned sot!' Houston cried. 'Why can't you be sober when I need you?'

Reardon, coming to life after being so roughly hauled out of the chair, started to draw back a big fist. Then he saw who it was.

'I'm sorry I lost my temper, Mike,' Houston said under his breath. 'But something serious has come up. That Jesse—have you seen him?'

Reardon blinked his eyes. 'He left here a while ago, Sam. Said he was going to do something but I forgot just what.'

'Try and remember,' Houston urged. 'It's important.'

'I recollect now. He was going home to pack for a trip somewhere. Then he had an

101

appointment with Barreras and Tweedy. Something about them buying out his wine stock.'

'That means he'll have his dealings with Burke Tweedy. Barreras has his headquarters in Saltillo.'

'Seems kind of funny, now that I think of it,' Mike Reardon said soberly, 'that Jesse would do business with a man he's threatened to kill.'

'Did Jesse tell you that?' Houston asked sharply.

'No, but it's all over town. Burke Tweedy claims that Jess is after him for some reason.'

'Because of Mrs. Tweedy, what else?'

Reardon looked around the tavern. A few of the patrons were regarding them curiously. 'I got a feeling Tweedy don't know about his wife and Jesse,' Reardon whispered.

'I can't believe Tweedy is that much of a fool.'

'Well, why would Tweedy say that Jesse threatened to kill him? And Tweedy no sooner gets that out of his mouth than he says he hopes buying the shipment of wine will sort of patch things up between them.'

Without waiting to hear more, Houston swung away from Reardon and hurried out into the street. This time he found Jesse Summer at home. 'What's this about you and Tweedy?' Houston wanted to know.

Jesse Summer looked harassed. 'He's offered

to buy me out, lock, stock and barrel.'

'There's talk that you threatened his life.'

'I would never do a thing like that,' Summer insisted.

'What time are you supposed to see Tweedy?'

'I'm late now for our appointment.'

At last the rage that Houston had been trying to control came to the surface. Shaking a long forefinger at his friend, he cried, 'Jesse, you're no damned good on earth!'

Jesse Summer went white. He stood his ground as Houston advanced as if to strike him in the face.

Houston thundered, 'I ought to beat your head off for ruining lives as you have!'

'I didn't realize what the consequences could be.' Looking up, gauging Houston's reaction, Jesse Summer said, 'Sam, God knows I didn't want it this way.'

'I don't suppose Burke Tweedy wanted it this way either.' Houston lowered the heavy fist he had lifted and beat it into the palm of his hand. 'Tweedy came to see me.' He recounted the office visit. 'I don't know whose murder he was talking about, yours or his.'

'He won't murder me. I have a pistol and I'll be armed at all times.' Summer turned and crossed the room to a small trunk. For a moment he was bent over, pawing through the contents. Then he straightened, a puzzled look in his eyes. 'The pistol is gone.'

'Is there some identifying mark on it?'

'My initials. On the grips.'

Houston looked grim. 'I have a feeling you'd better get out of town. Now!'

There was a sudden sound of voices in the alley, of men moving toward the building, then a banging on the door. 'Open up, Summer!'

Houston flung the door open. There were about twenty men in the alley. At sight of Houston, they looked surprised.

The spokesman, a man named Tobin whom Houston had whipped in court on a land script fraud, wore a small man's smile of triumph. 'Houston, we're looking for your friend Jesse Summer.'

'For what reason?' Houston blocked the doorway so the men couldn't see inside the room.

'He just shot and killed Burke Tweedy.'

'How is that possible?' Houston said. 'I've been here with Summer for some time. Step out, Jesse.'

When Summer appeared, some of the men exchanged glances.

But Tobin said, 'Summer must have just got here. He ran all the way from the Tweedy place.'

'No,' Houston said.

'You'd protect a scallywag like Summer? It was his gun that killed Tweedy.'

'You have proof?'

104

'Summer's initials on the grips. I have it figured out, Houston. They quarreled and Summer shot him, then got nervous and dropped his gun and fled here—'

'That's no proof.'

'Tweedy left a note,' Tobin said triumphantly. 'He said if anything happened to him to look for Jesse Summer.'

'Just a moment, gentlemen.' A woman's dead voice spoke, and all heads turned.

Hats came whipping off as Iris Tweedy came along the alley. Her bloodless face bore no expression. She did not lift her gaze to Jesse Summer standing in the doorway.

'My husband stole Jesse Summer's pistol. He planned to take his own life and have Jesse hanged for the crime. He wedged the pistol in a door, then touched the trigger with the tip of a walking stick. He thought I had gone out, but I hadn't. I saw him do it, but could not prevent the act.'

'It's only your word,' Tobin snarled. 'Everybody knows that you and Jesse Summer—'

'Tobin, shut your mouth!' Houston's voice thundered and the look of fury on his face caused Tobin to back up.

Iris Tweedy, still without looking up, said, 'My husband—my late husband—could never make me with child. Another man did. My late husband could not stand the ridicule he knew

105

would follow if such a thing ever got out. Many things he couldn't face up to—most of all his life.'

Turning, she walked back down the alley. And Jesse Summer suddenly pushed past Houston. He caught up with her, while the men looked on.

'Iris, I want to marry you—'

'I am a widow now, Mr. Summer,' she said, turning the pale face to his. 'I am going to hire servants. They will have orders that if you try and trespass on my property you are to be shot dead. Is that understood?'

Without waiting for a reply, she gathered her skirts and majestically made her way to the street.

Tobin tried to rouse the crowd. 'No matter what Summer does Houston defends him!'

'You are wrong,' Houston cut in coldly. All eyes were on his commanding figure. 'If Jesse Summer had killed Burke Tweedy, I would have seen that he hanged for it.'

Jesse Summer's shoulders stiffened when he heard this. Slowly the men drifted along the alley, talking among themselves, casting sidelong glances back at Summer.

When they were alone again, Jesse Summer said, 'I hate to think what would have happened to me if you hadn't come along and I had kept that appointment with Tweedy. I'd have been on the scene of the supposed crime, with my gun the death weapon. Sam, I'll make this up to you one day.'

'The only way you can make it up to me is to stay out of my sight. I hope I never lay eyes on you again as long as I live!'

Turning his back, Sam Houston strode away.

CHAPTER NINE

Conditions in Texas grew worse during the next few months, with Santa Anna's arrogance toward the province daily becoming more pronounced. Some of those in the Jackson camp, failing in the attempts to purchase Texas, were now openly trying to embroil her in revolution over the matter of Austin's arrest.

But Houston managed to quell the flames before they plunged this last outpost of the Mexican Republic into disaster.

Conditions eased somewhat when Austin was released from prison. But due to the harsh treatment he received he was a broken man. When this became known the old resentment against Mexico was intensified.

One day Houston told a group in a Nacogdoches tavern that he had received a letter from Mexico City. 'Santa Anna is hard-pressed. His own people are threatening to revolt.'

'Looks like the Mexicans will handle Santa Anna to suit themselves,' said Mike Reardon. 'Our troubles are over.'

Houston shook his head. '*El Presidente* knows the only chance to save his regime is to take the minds of his people off his own corruption.'

'Just how does he figure to do that, Sam?'

'He's looking for an excuse to march against us.'

Men exchanged glances. 'You sure about that, Sam?'

'As sure as Sunday. Boys, we'd better get ready for a fight.'

Soon the pressures increased. Gunfire was exchanged between Mexican troops and Texas settlers. These events Houston knew, were designed to force Texas to revolt, which would give Santa Anna all the excuse needed to launch a full-scale offensive.

A skirmish at Gonzales brought matters to a head. Two days later the citizens of Nacogdoches held a mass meeting in the street. A vote was quickly taken and the results announced.

'Sam Houston has been elected commander-in-chief of the forces of eastern Texas!' was the cry that swept the town.

Thanking them for their confidence in him, one of Houston's first acts was to issue an appeal for recruits. 'Volunteers are invited to join our ranks with a good rifle and one

108

hundred rounds of ammunition ... Liberty or Death!'

Abandoning his law practice, Houston flung himself wholeheartedly into the task before him, even though he did feel personally that the revolution was premature.

'The Mexicans are good soldiers,' he said to a crowd. 'Don't feel yourselves that we can stand up to them unless we have sufficient training in warfare.'

Already Santa Anna had sent his brother-in-law, General Martín Perfecto Cos, to handle the trouble in Texas.

$$\star \quad \star \quad \star$$

The settlers moved swiftly. In November a convention of fifty-five delegates was held at San Felipe. Houston put aside the fancy uniform, befitting his rank, he had ordered from New Orleans. In his old buckskins he was easily the most dominant figure at the convention.

'The one thing I desire most,' Houston told Jim Bowie, 'is Texas independence. Or annexation to the United States.'

The sandy-haired Bowie took another drink from a bottle he had been nursing most of the afternoon. The loss of his wife and two children in a plague that swept Mexico had left him stunned.

Drawing his Bowie knife, the frontiersman shouted, 'Down with Santa Anna!' And the cry was taken up by the others.

A constitution was framed and among those named to the General Council was Stephen F. Austin, who had returned from Mexico. Henry Smith was named governor. With only one dissenting vote Houston was elected commander-in-chief of the Texas armies.

Houston's first move was to dislodge General Cos, who was firmly entrenched at San Antonio de Bexar. Busy planning the over-all strategy for the war, Houston put the Bexar campaign in other hands.

It was Mike Reardon whom Houston sent to Bexar with the warning, 'Keep your eyes and ears open. I have enemies, Mike. Let me know if any of them attempt to jeopardize our efforts just to strike back at me.'

Reardon, his beard foul, his eyes bloodshot, saluted and rode away, his head throbbing at each step of the horse. The previous night he had seen the bottom of numerous jugs with Jim Bowie. These days Bowie seemed to have an unlimited capacity for any sort of liquid fire being sold on the frontier.

There was an excuse for Bowie, Reardon told himself. When you have a beautiful wife and two handsome children cut down by some foul disease, it is enough to unsettle a man's mind.

It was Houston's contention that Cos should

be starved out of Bexar by surrounding the town. Stephen Austin, at the battle site, also echoed Houston's caution. The Texans had five hundred troops while General Cos had more than one thousand well-trained regulars and artillery. To waste the lives of Texans against a town as well fortified as Bexar would be foolhardy, Houston believed. The buildings were of stone and adobe and could easily be defended. Furthermore, Houston held the opinion the town could not be taken without cannon, which his army lacked.

Many times Mike Reardon had heard Houston discuss the situation at San Antonio de Bexar. But when Reardon finally arrived at the Texan camp he found little evidence of discipline, only wild confusion.

One segment of the Texas army wanted to engage the Mexicans immediately. Colonel Frank Johnson was one of those clamoring for an assault on the town.

Ben Milam, who had once been imprisoned by the Mexicans, was impatient to seek vengeance. Those urging immediate attack included James Fannin, a Georgian, whose reckless nature abhorred inactivity. Also in camp was Deaf Smith, a squat, heavily built man, and one of the best scouts.

Hardly had Reardon dismounted amid the confusion than a man shouted, 'Mike, you old rascal!'

Turning, Reardon saw that it was Jesse Summer, garbed in shabby buckskins in place of the fancy attire he had worn at Nacogdoches.

'Jesse!' Reardon slapped Summer on the back. 'I figured you'd be dead by now.'

A wan smile touched Summer's lips. 'I can only attribute my continued good health to this age of poor marksmanship. On the part of husbands, at least.'

They moved away from the road where a wagon was careening, the driver lashing the team. Riders saddled up and moved out and others came in. Men were lined up at cook fires. There were tents and piles of supplies all over the area.

Jesse Summer's handsome face showed incipient lines and there was more gray at his temples. 'Have you seen Sam lately?' he asked Reardon.

'He sent me down here,' Reardon answered.

'I hear he's bearing the whole burden of the fight. How's he holding up?'

'Sam's toting Texas on one hand and fighting off the politicians on the other.' Reardon dug a fingernail through the tangle of long black hair and scratched his head. 'Sam figured to get an army together before we do much fighting. But . . .' Reardon waved a square hand at the motley crew of volunteers who were clamoring for action. 'They've smelled blood,' Reardon went on. 'It's liable to end up like Horseshoe Bend.'

Summer looked around at the disorganized units. 'This time with the massacre on our side, not the enemy's.' He shook his head disconsolately.

'They oughta listen to Sam,' Reardon said firmly.

A familiar figure stepped around a wagon. Jim Bowie, his oversize knife swinging at his belt, strode up. He lifted a hand to Reardon, then said, 'Why isn't Houston here? What good's a general if he don't figure to fight?'

Reardon flushed at this insult to Houston. 'Sam claims it's going to be a long war. This is just one battle. If we get tromped on by them Mexicans, there's going to be a lot of weeping widows.'

Jim Bowie's face changed. 'My widow won't weep.' Turning, he marched off, the wind tearing at his sandy hair.

Jesse Summer said, 'He's mighty touchy these days. I have a feeling he's going to come to a violent end.'

Reardon shrugged. 'Say, did you ever see the Tweedy woman again?'

'The baby died,' Summer said grimly. 'Iris is running the freight line with Barreras. I once tried to see her. She sent some teamsters after me. It was a week before I could walk.'

'How come she turned against you so?'

'I guess when Tweedy shot himself she just froze up inside toward all men.'

'She was a pretty woman, Jesse. Sure funny about a fella like Tweedy. Why'd he marry her in the first place?'

'Something we'll never know. He wanted me to be hanged.' Summer felt of his throat. 'If it hadn't been for Sam—' He tried to swallow a tautness. 'If you see him, Mike, tell him hello.'

When Reardon saw another old friend in the crowd of armed men, Jesse Summer walked off. This talk of Sam Houston and Iris Tweedy had depressed him. In Nacogdoches he had seen her from a distance, her hair cut short, dressed like a man, her beauty gone. She looked like a tough, red-haired trail hand. And there was no one to blame but himself.

The sun breaking through the clouds beat against the white-walled buildings of the town. A Texan was staring through a spyglass at something. Turning, the man handed the glass to Summer. 'Take a look,' he said. 'That'll make you itch.'

Through the glass Summer saw a Mexican gunner beside a cannon on the wall of the abandoned mission, the Alamo. The gunner had his arm around the waist of a pretty girl. Her blouse had slipped low about her breasts. She was pointing at the Texans, screaming something Summer couldn't hear.

The long-jawed Texan who owned the glass said, 'I hear there's a house in Bexar where they got fifty girls for them Mex soldiers. Makes me itch just to think about it. I'll kill me some Mexicans, then I'll make them girls squeal.'

'A worthy ambition,' Jesse Summer said sourly.

As he moved disconsolately among the troops, he sensed their growing restlessness. And he couldn't blame them. God knew he was edgy himself. For weeks they had been sitting around, waiting for the supplies of General Cos to run low, waiting for the white flag of surrender to be raised.

As he neared a mud-splattered wagon he saw Captain Fannin arguing with Bowie. 'Houston's a fool to wait,' Fannin said. 'We can't hold these men back much longer.'

Reinforcements arrived, among them the New Orleans Grays and a company from Mobile.

'I ain't scared of no Mex in the world,' one of the newcomers said, shaking his fist at the town.

'You'd better learn to be,' Summer said drily. 'The Mexicans are good fighters.'

'You talk like a Mex lover for sure.'

'And you talk like a fool.'

The man, larger than Summer, doubled his fists, but Mike Reardon said, 'Enough of that.' The stranger took one look at Reardon's formidable size, and backed off. Reardon said, 'Lucky you didn't press him, mister. Jesse Summer don't fight with his fists.'

'Thanks, Mike,' Summer said. 'We need every man. Be a shame if we were shy one.' He jerked a thumb at the stranger. 'Even him.'

Some of the men laughed, and the tension was gone.

On November 25, Austin turned over the army at Bexar to Edward Burleson, and left for his new post as commissioner to the United States.

And when Burleson made no move to attack, some of the men said, 'He's scared of them Mexicans.'

'Listen to this,' Summer said. 'Cos has cannon in the main plaza covering every approach. He's fortified the Alamo.'

A boy with a wispy mustache, who was eating boiled beef with the others for the evening meal, whooped with laughter. 'We'll steal them Mex cannon.'

'Not so easy,' Summer said.

As the days passed, he grew more restless with the others. And Mike Reardon, who had bragged, 'I don't aim to take one drink till Cos surrenders,' now resumed his old habits under the mounting pressure. To make matters worse, the troops began to quarrel among themselves.

Summer saw disgusted men ride away to their homes. There was the growing threat of wholesale desertions.

On December 4, word was passed that there

116

would be a retirement to winter quarters. This was too much.

Ben Milam, still aching for revenge against the Mexicans who had once imprisoned him, cried, 'Who will go with Old Ben Milam into San Antonio?'

Hardly had the words died than volunteers were springing forward. Rifle under his arm, Jesse Summer moved to join those who would go with Milam.

Mike Reardon, not to be outdone, said, 'Count me in.'

Under cover of darkness, Jesse Summer and the other volunteers moved up closer to the town, where they huddled in the December cold. As the first thread of dawn light appeared on the horizon, the Texans sprang to life. With Milam at the head of one division and Colonel Frank Johnson at the other, they made their charge.

As Summer ran, the rifle slick in his hands despite the cold, he thought, *If I hadn't been such a fool in Nacogdoches I could be part of Sam Houston's government—not here where I very likely will throw my useless life away.*

The feeling that he might not live out the engagement intensified when a raking fire suddenly burst upon them. He realized then that the Mexican sentinels were not fooled as the Texans had hoped.

Round shot whistled down the narrow streets. Summer felt the cold beef he had eaten for breakfast rise dangerously into his throat when he saw a racing Texan suddenly lose the top of his head.

All round him now was wild confusion as the Texans were trapped in the deadly streets. The boy with the wispy mustache sat against a stone wall, dazedly staring at a splinter of bone protruding from his torn buckskins.

Seeking to pull the boy to shelter, Summer leaped for him. A bullet caught the boy in the side of the head, and there was no longer in the dead mind any concern for a shattered arm.

Ben Milam's voice rose above the roar of the guns. 'Follow me, boys! Into this house!'

Stout Texas shoulders caved in a wooden door. As they streamed into the stone-walled house, Summer saw great yellow-brown clouds of smoke rising from the cannon in the main plaza.

A round shot struck the building a glancing blow. The whole place shook under the impact. If they could survive here for any length of time at all, they might make it.

Mike Reardon, his face smeared with powder smoke, said, 'Some of the boys are in another house yonder.' He waved to his right. 'But there's a lot of dead ones.'

For the next three days Jesse Summer thought his eardrums would never be free of the sound of cannon fire. Day and night they stood with rifles at the windows, their eyes smarting from the smoke, watching the advancing waves of troops, then the withdrawal, leaving the dead.

It was Ben Milam's plan to consolidate the Texas forces by using crowbars to smash their way to the house where Johnson and his men were holed up.

For hours they battered their way from one house to another, some taking turns with the crowbars while others heaped a devastating fire on the troops seeking to dislodge them.

'We got 'em now, boys!' Ben Milam shouted triumphantly, and fell forward, shot through the head by a stray bullet.

'They got Old Ben!' was the cry that went up.

Driven almost to a frenzy now, the Texans slowly pushed their way from house to house toward the plaza, battering walls, smashing through doors and windows. So tired they could hardly stand, they doggedly wielded the heavy crowbars.

Finally they reached a position where they could cover the fortified plaza with the wicked, enfilading fire of their rifles. Just as they were about to close in, Summer saw to his amazement that General Cos, abandoning his dead, was withdrawing to the Alamo.

That night Deaf Smith, who had been on a scouting mission, returned to the battered, weary Texans with grim news. Mexican reinforcements had marched to Cos' relief. 'At least five hundred of 'em,' Smith announced.

'We don't care if it's five thousand!' cried Reardon.

'That makes no sense,' Jesse Summer said wearily. 'We're less than three hundred.'

But Reardon was nudging him. 'Look!' He was pointing at a white flag being raised above the Alamo.

Beaming with pleasure, Colonel Johnson and some of his men went to arrange the terms of surrender. With reinforcements or not, General Cos had had enough of the maniacal sharpshooting Texans.

When Cos and his thousand men marched out, agreeing never again to take up arms against Texas, a great shout went up. 'We won the war! We won the war!'

All restraint brought on by a semblance of military order gave way. The Texans went wild. Even those wounded who were able to hobble about joined in the tumult.

A disheveled Mike Reardon, his buckskins ripped by a Mexican sword, turned unerringly toward a supply of whisky. He found a jug half-buried under a collapsed wall.

'I been here before, Jesse,' Reardon said, as they shared the jug. 'There's a place where the girls are. I'm going to see if they're still there. Come on, we'll have ourselves a time. We've earned it, that's for sure.'

Jesse Summer looked down at himself and wrinkled his nose. 'You go ahead, Mike. I've got to clean up.'

Reardon grinned. 'They'll love you just as you are, Jesse. You're still a handsome, no-good—' Reardon slapped him on the back and staggered off, drinking from his jug.

A search through the rubble brought Summer at last to a well. Using a bucket, he managed to wash and shave. Somewhat refreshed and feeling a little less like an unbathed renegade, he prowled the town. A detail was hauling away the dead in carts. A drunken soldier was shooting at a bloodied Mexican garrison cap lying in the street.

Passing an abandoned house with a crumpled wall, Summer saw brown fingers with pink nails flat against a buckskin-clad back. He couldn't see the girl hidden by the brawny form of the Texan. But he caught a flash of her petticoats folded back like the petals of a flower. And he heard the girl's deep sigh of pleasure.

He thought of the Texan who'd had the spyglass and how he had watched the girl on the wall of the Alamo. 'I'll make them squeal,' the man had said. Just two blocks away Summer had seen him being lifted into a burial cart.

On through the town he roamed, the oily smell of gunsmoke still tainting the air. He saw other Texans in houses and heard the giggles of women and thought that this was as it had always been: welcome to the conquerors.

At last he came to a stone house with many rooms where the laughter of the women sounded more professional.

A voice thickened from liquor cried, 'Jesse, in here!'

Summer pushed his way through a noisy, crowded parlor. He followed the sound of the voice that continued to call his name, finally coming to a narrow room with a window overlooking the street. A faded tapestry hid the cracks in one wall.

He saw a very young, very pale girl sitting on a pile of blankets in a corner. And somehow he was reminded of the sorry bed in his own quarters at Nacogdoches.

Beside the girl, a thick arm about her waist, sat Mike Reardon. He was just uncorking a fresh jug. His eyes did not quite focus.

'This here's my prize,' Reardon said happily giving the girl a squeeze. 'How do you like my prize, Jesse?'

'*Buenas tardes, Señorita*,' Summer said, giving the girl a slight bow.

She did not speak. Her dark eyes were fixed on him. She kept biting her full lips.

'You do not belong in this place,' Summer said to her in Spanish. 'You seem frightened.'

'I belong here.' She looked at the floor. She had small breasts and seemed quite frail. He judged she was not more than fifteen.

Reardon drank, spilling whisky down the front of his buckskin shirt. 'You come back in an hour, Jesse. You're my friend. I share whisky and my girls with my friends.'

In another room a woman laughed shrilly. A man cursed and sent a jug hurtling through the front door. It landed with a crash in the street, and set a mongrel dog to barking.

Summer looked at the girl, indicating the drunken Reardon with a nod of his head. 'He's paying you?'

'*Sí.*' She lowered her eyes.

'You have been with a man before?'

'No—never.' Her fingers were clenching at the material of her full skirt. One of Reardon's large hands disappeared and the girl looked stricken. She got up, her body stiffened. She leaned against the wall, her eyes closed for a moment. Then she looked at Summer.

'You will go, *por favor,*' she said.

Reardon said, 'She don't talk nothing but Mex, Jesse. You tell her I said she was to be nice to you. But you come back in an hour. I got money, Jesse. I buy her for you.'

In the street somebody fired a gun and howled wildly, and a man said, 'Take that pistol away from him. He's loco!'

Summer touched the girl's thin arm. 'You *want* to do this?'

'No.'

'Then you have a family. They are hungry.

You do it for them.'

'It is my sister. She owns this house. She says this night I become a woman. It is time I work, she says.'

Jesse Summer felt a great disgust for the human race.

He said, 'Wait here, Mike. I'll get you a girl.'

Reardon just blinked at him, uncomprehending. In the hall, Summer looked toward the crowded parlor. A girl tossing her hips came along the hall and saw him. She had a quick, white-toothed smile.

Taking his hands, she placed them on her breasts. 'You like?'

'Yes. I have a friend. I want to make him a present.'

Her eyes darkened dangerously. 'You do not like me for yourself, but for your friend? What is that matter with you? You are one of those—a butterfly?'

She laughed and Summer said, 'I am man enough, believe me.'

Taking her by the hand he led her into the room. Reardon still sat on the bed, holding his jug. The girl had her back to the wall.

Summer jerked his head at her. 'Run,' he said, 'while you have the chance.'

But the girl just stood there. She seemed more frightened than ever now that Summer had brought the other girl into the room.

124

Summer forced a smile. 'Mike, I'll trade you.'

Reardon took one look at the new girl and shook his head. 'I don't want that scum!'

'I mean it, Mike,' Summer said seriously.

Reardon looked at him, his eyes slightly crossed, then he set the jug on the floor and stood up. In the small room he seemed enormous. 'Jesse, you're trying to steal from me.'

'No, listen to me, Mike—'

Reardon's fist came flying like one of the crowbars that had been used to smash doors. Even though Summer stepped back, avoiding the full force of the blow, he was knocked against the wall. Before he could recover Reardon was on him. And as they struggled, he heard the girl say sharply, 'Come, Luz. These two wish to fight, not do the other!'

Summer was slammed to the floor. He managed to lift a knee as Reardon came down. Reardon gave a grunt of pain and rolled aside. Then Summer was on his feet, and as Reardon came up, he hit him on the side of the face. Reardon's maniacal expression did not alter.

'Goddamn you, Jesse! I'll kill you!'

He reached for the Bowie knife at his belt, and as it came free, Summer made a desperate lunge for the wrist. His fingers closed on it and the weight of his body dragged Reardon off balance. They fell across the bed, the knife clattering to the floor.

As they broke apart Summer sprang to his feet. Reardon tried to wrap his arms about Summer's waist and drag him down.

Leaping free, Summer struck him hard on the point of the jaw. With a sigh Reardon went down and lay still.

Dazed, his knuckles aching, Summer reeled out into the hall. The place was even more crowded than before. Frantically he searched for the girl, remembering her name.

'Luz!'

Some fifteen minutes later he finally saw the older girl he had brought to exchange for Luz. In the howling mob of Texans he cried, 'Where is Luz?'

'Earning money—where she should be.'

Summer saw a door open down the hall and Luz came out with a soldier. Then another caught her by the arm and led her back into the room.

Shaking his head, Summer returned to the room where he had left Reardon. The man was just coming to.

Grinning, Summer said, 'Forgive me, Mike.'

Reardon rubbed a hand over his split lips. His eyes were ugly. 'Get out of here, Jesse!'

'I was wrong, I guess. There is no chance of halting the inevitable. By now the girl is obviously well indoctrinated.'

Reardon staggered to his feet. 'You bastard!'

Summer spread his hands. 'Understand,

126

Mike. I guess it was some stupid noble impulse. Maybe an urge to try and undo some of my wrongs with a good deed.'

'Sam Houston's got no use for you, Jesse. Neither have I. You ever come around me again and I'll kill you!'

Brushing past Summer, almost knocking him down with a shoulder, Reardon left the room. After a moment Summer went out into the street, that was still filled with boisterous soldiers celebrating their victory. As he walked through the darkness a great sadness touched him.

CHAPTER TEN

The victory at San Antonia de Bexar caused all of Texas to go wild. Everywhere Houston went he heard the shout: 'We whipped the Mexicans!'

Even the members of the Council were overcome with enthusiasm. 'The Republic is secure!'

Houston's booming voice tried to infect them with realism. 'Santa Anna will avenge the defeat of General Cos!'

But one of the members countered with, 'Santa Anna will never dare set foot on Texas soil!'

'Listen to me,' Houston urged. 'What we need is an army.'

'We have an army. They defeated Cos at Bexar.'

'Our boys fought valiantly. But Cos made blunders. Santa Anna is not so liable to repeat his brother-in-law's mistakes.'

'One Texan is worth a hundred Mexicans!'

'That attitude will bury us,' Houston warned. Then trying to stem his rising temper, he added, 'What we need are trained men.'

'My God, Houston!' cried a Council member. 'Can't you get it through your head that the war is over? Why in hell do we need an army?'

Houston drew himself up. 'The war has just begun.'

Houston knew that his prestige had suffered from the victory at Bexar—because it had been his theory, shared by others, that Bexar could not be captured without artillery. He had wanted the siege to drag on until he had time to build a formidable fighting force.

There was even a move afoot to displace Houston as commander-in-chief. This cry for Houston's removal stemmed largely from a Scottish surgeon named James Grant, whose holdings near Matamoros had been seized by the Mexican government. Grant, in trying to arouse sympathy for a campaign against Matamoros, painted glowing tales of plunder should volunteers follow him below the Rio Grande.

After listening to a delegation of Grant supporters at his headquarters, Houston said, 'Our army is not in the business of rescuing the confiscated property of Dr. Grant.'

'He's a citizen!'

'As citizens we must not scatter our forces. We must build an army big enough to meet Santa Anna head on.'

On Christmas Day Houston moved his headquarters to Washington on the Brazos, a collection of huts flanking one street. More headaches came his way as he tried to whip his volunteers into a semblance of a fighting force.

A courier brought him a dispatch: 'Grant is headed for Matamoros with two hundred men, among them the crack New Orleans Grays.'

'What next!' Houston cried, shaking his fist at the rough board ceiling of his headquarters. 'It seems that everything from the shoeing of a horse to leading an army is in my hands.'

Buckling on his sword, Houston rode after Grant in a driving rain, finally overtaking him January 14, 1836, at Goliad.

While arguing with the adamant Grant, Houston received further shocking news. Troops led by Santa Anna had crossed the Rio Grande.

This was a stunning blow. Houston had not expected an invasion until spring. 'I didn't think Santa Anna was capable of moving an army in the dead of winter.' He knew that many of those in the Texas government had been so busy wrangling among themselves they hadn't realized Santa Anna's ominous shadow was to darken their own republic.

'What do we do now, General?' asked a frightened resident of Goliad.

'We can't waste time crying over past mistakes,' he responded and went to call on Jim Bowie, who was in Goliad at the time.

'Looks like we're about to have some shooting, Sam,' Bowie said.

'That's an understatement. Jim, I want you to take a handful of men to San Antonio de Bexar. Demolish the fortifications. Remove all the cannon.'

'That will be easy,' Bowie drawled. 'Anything else?'

'Yes. Be sure you blow up the Alamo and abandon the place.'

*　　　*　　　*

It was shortly after Bowie rode off to round up his men that Houston received a direct slap from the Council. They had deposed Governor Smith. Houston's advice concerning a Matamoros campaign had been ignored. James W. Fannin was to head up the army that was to take Matamoros.

Houston went white when he received the

dispatch from the Council. 'I wash my hands of this,' he said heavily.

Days went by and as Santa Anna moved north, panic increased. And there was a rising sentiment among the settlers that Houston had been unfairly treated. With war an actuality he was needed more than ever. William Barret Travis and a handful of men were now holding out against Santa Anna at the Alamo.

Houston had disappeared, going for a time 'back to my Indians.'

But he was ready when a convention was called. On March 1, in a frame shanty at Washington on the Brazos, fifty-eight duly elected representatives of the people of Texas were assembled in somber silence. Their task was to frame a declaration of independence.

'We must demand complete separation from Mexico,' Houston told the delegates.

And when the document itself was signed, it was unanimously agreed that Houston once again be made commander-in-chief.

As he saw all eyes look his way hopefully, in his heart there was an urge to flay these men for their own stupidity. Many of them had previously humiliated him by declining his advice. Yet in their desperation they turned to him again.

'Houston, will you accept the honor?'

'Gentlemen, I accept.'

While a norther swept in, dropping the

temperature to just above freezing, a messenger arrived with a last appeal from Travis and his men at the Alamo. 'The spirits of my men are still high, although they have had much to depress them ... I hope your honorable body will hasten on reinforcements.'

Mingled anger and panic swept Washington. A motion was made that 'the convention do immediately adjourn and march to the relief of the Alamo.'

But Houston held them in check. 'Unless our declaration of independence is backed up by a sound government,' he thundered, 'we are nothing but a mob. I urge you to elect officials, and set up the necessary machinery of administration.'

As Houston snatched his hat from a peg, one of the delegates said, 'And where do you go, Houston?'

'To the Alamo. Where else in hell did you think I'd be going!'

With three volunteers he rode out of Washington, the chill wind stinging his face. His Indian coat and buckskin vest barely kept out the cold.

One of the volunteers rode close. 'I thought you gave Jim Bowie orders to blow up the Alamo and clear out.'

Houston swallowed a hard lump in his throat. 'Good men are dying there. It's not time to dwell on what should have been done. We'll

132

find men at Gonzales to help us.'

'I hope we'll be in time to save the Alamo.'

'If God smiles on Texas this day we will.'

As Houston skirted a forest he saw an eagle sail into the bitter sky, screaming. And the Cherokee heart of Houston turned black with despair.

★   ★   ★

The news that Santa Anna had crossed the Rio Grande had reached Mike Reardon some days earlier. Seeking to volunteer in Houston's command, he tried for several days to learn where his companion in arms from the Horseshoe Bend days could be found. While hunting for Houston he met a trapper friend, Jeremiah Zebb. At Zebb's cabin they drank to the future of Texas and wondered darkly just how they could help stave off what seemed to be the inevitable.

Reardon said bitterly, 'Houston wanted an army. They wouldn't give him one. Now look what's happened.'

Zebb, a stringy man in dirty buckskin, snored at the table.

The sounds of an approaching wagon roused Reardon. He staggered outside. The wagon, driven by a harassed man wearing a bearskin coat, pulled up at sight of Reardon. He accepted the jug Reardon handed him.

133

'What's the news, friend?' Reardon asked.

'Travis and Bowie pulled outa Bexar,' the man said, taking another drink and returning the jug to Reardon. 'Them and their men have holed up in the Alamo. Santa Anna's got 'em surrounded.'

Reardon fingered his black beard. 'Reckon I better go give them boys a hand.'

The man on the wagon seat shook his head. 'Nobody can help them. I'm running. So's most everybody else. You better do the same. Mex cavalry is prowling the country.'

When the wagon had gone Reardon lurched back into the cabin where Zebb still snored. Reardon got his rifle and drunkenly saddled his horse as best he could. As he rode away from the Zebb cabin he felt as if the furies had nested in his stomach. He'd had little to eat, being more interested in emptying the jugs Zebb had stored away.

After many miles he came upon an abandoned cabin with a scrawny cow wandering about. He shot the animal and butchered it. He made a fire and roasted what meat he could eat and carry, and left the remainder. He hated to waste food, but there was nothing else he could do under the circumstances. He had to fight for Texas. This couldn't be done on an empty belly.

He pushed on again, the meat he had eaten and the knifing wind finally sobering him.

If he needed anything else to sober him, he got it when he neared Bexar. Everywhere he looked he saw Mexican troops. Now he could hear the rattle of gunfire, the deep boom of cannon. At each shot he grew sicker. He knew that Travis, according to the fleeing settler, had only a handful of men.

In the distance Reardon saw great clouds of smoke rise above the town. Keeping out of sight of Mexican patrols, he desperately tried to find a way to go to Travis' aid. But at the moment the Alamo seemed sealed off by enemy troops.

Then on March 1, a party of thirty-two colonists, under the command of Captain J. W. Smith, arrived from Gonzales. They came upon Reardon standing disconsolately beside the road.

'Where you boys headed?' Reardon asked.

'We're going to get into the Alamo and help Travis.'

'How about one more man?'

'You're more than welcome.'

The Mexicans were so intent on the siege of the Alamo that they had neglected their rear, obviously not expecting trouble. They had scouts out, looking for the approach of a sizable Texas army. Reardon had nearly run into them while making up his mind what to do.

Hats tipped against the sun, the thirty-four men came up quietly behind the Mexicans.

After scouting the area, they found a gap in the Santa Anna lines. Utilizing this corridor, they swiftly approached. And suddenly the bewildered Mexicans were faced with a yelling, shooting pack of Texans.

An officer berated his men, trying to swing around one of the cannons to slaughter the onrushing Texans. He went down. Mexican troops fell back on all sides under the furious charge. Swords dripped red.

From the walls of the Alamo, where fourteen small guns had been placed, Travis and his men shouted encouragement. They poured their own fire into the ranks of Mexicans.

At last the barred gates were opened wide enough to permit the entry of the sprinting Gonzales men. There was wide acclaim as the defenders of the Alamo gathered around the newcomers. Davy Crockett laid aside his rifle and picked up his fiddle. All through the night those '*loco Americanos*,' as the Mexicans called them, danced and jigged and shouted to the squeaky fiddle.

Reardon was shocked at the appearance of Jim Bowie, whose eyes burned with the fever of typhoid pneumonia that had ravaged his body. Bowie tried to laugh with the others from where he lay on his cot.

During the next few days the rations grew slim, and the powder-streaked faces grew grim and gaunt as the men tightened their belts. On this frontier they were used to such things as slim rations, for a man was sometimes forced to go for considerable periods without food.

Poor food, and little of that, and a failing supply of ammunition was bad enough. A still greater enemy within was lack of sleep. For twenty-four hours a day they had to be alert, for the Mexicans from time to time would assault the walls, then withdraw, leaving their dead.

Gradually the mounting pressures, the lack of sleep and food, the growing realization that time was running out on them took its toll of the Texans. They began to stagger, drugged from the ceaseless battle to keep awake and to sustain life in their bodies.

No matter what the time of day or night, a call from the sentries would bring them springing from their pallets to man the walls. Their marksmanship took a dreadful toll of the enemy, but there were always more Mexicans to replace those killed in the assaults.

So tired he could hardly keep his eyes open, his mind fuzzy, Reardon was on hand when a courier named Bonham returned to the Alamo. Days before he had managed to slip through Santa Anna's lines and push a horse in a wild ride to Goliad. There he had appealed to Fannin to lead his crack troops to their aid.

Hollow-eyed, on the verge of exhaustion, Bonham now gave Travis his report. There was no hope of Fannin bringing aid. His wagons had mired down and some of his oxen had taken sick and died.

That night Travis called a meeting in the nave of the old mission church. The haggard Texans stood quietly, waiting. Beyond the walls there was a lull in the firing. The air was biting cold.

Travis, his blue eyes bloodshot from strain and lack of sleep, his red hair a tangle, addressed his men. 'It doesn't look like we're going to get much help. Listen to me.' Travis looked around at the gaunt defenders of Texas freedom. 'Bonham was able to slip through Santa Anna's lines and so were you boys from Gonzales. There's a fair chance that any who want to leave can get through. You might make it under cover of darkness, if you leave one at a time.'

When Travis finished, the men exchanged glances, but none made any reply. Some leaned tiredly against the sacred walls. Others rested their weight on rifles.

Clearing his throat, Travis went on, 'It won't be any reflection on your honor if you go now. God knows you've held off Santa Anna for nine days and nights. You Gonzales men, you've all got families.'

'Not me,' Mike Reardon said. 'I come in with them boys, but I got nobody. Speaking for myself, I'm staying.'

Reardon heard a shout go up from the others.

And when the yelling tapered off into abrupt silence, the men looked around at each other. And they all knew they had sentenced themselves to death.

Jim Bowie, who had insisted he be carried into the nave of the church on his cot, so as not to miss the meeting, lay with his eyes closed. His clothing fit loosely, the disease having shrunken his great frame. The fingers of each thin hand gripped a loaded pistol.

'Me too, boys,' Bowie said. 'I'll stay with you to the last.'

During the day a breeze came up, whipping the red flag above the Mexican positions—the flag of no quarter. And the Mexican bugles again sounded the *deguelle* that also signified no prisoners were to be taken.

In the days that followed, the Mexicans kept up a steady bombardment. By sheer force of will and excellent shooting, the Texans were able to stave off the repeated assaults on the gates. So intense was the feeling among the defenders that even the badly wounded—those still able to walk after a fashion—refused to give up their rifles. They stumbled, half-fell or crawled to their positions on the walls when the sentries cried, 'Here they come again!'

Every man knew that each sortie might be the last one they could repulse.

It finally came—the inevitable. In the

pitch-black darkness a sentinel suddenly cried out a warning.

Roused from drugged sleep, the men staggered to their positions.

Reardon, half-asleep, was shocked violently awake, when from his post on the wall, he peered down at the great mass of advancing troops. There was a shadowy wave of movement, the ominous clank of scaling ladders thudding against the walls, chilling the blood. Because the troops were already at the walls, Texas cannon were useless. Only the gun that Travis fired from the convent roof was still effective.

Under the raking fire of Texas rifles, wave after wave of Mexicans were cut down. But still they pressed forward, with guns from their own troops trained at their backs to prevent retreat. Mexicans hurled themselves forward with the recklessness of the doomed, only to be met by the stunning fire from the walls. Finally by weight of sheer numbers they were able to breach the walls.

Reardon saw them pour through like an onrushing tide that has burst a dam. He saw Travis collapse, dying as he propelled a last cannon shot down into the screaming horde.

At the door to the church, Crockett was overwhelmed and the others were forced back. As troops swarmed in, Reardon tried to reach Jim Bowie, but was cut off.

Bowie, still lying on his cot, bared his teeth,

and emptied both pistols into the faces of those who would murder him in his bed. Then he was engulfed.

In the narrow confines of the church the din was deafening. Like an automaton, Reardon fired his rifle, reloaded and fired again. Then his last shot struck the jaw of a Mexican soldier. As the man crumpled, Reardon tried to reload. But he was an island surrounded by a sea of dark faces shouting Spanish oaths.

From a corner of his eye he saw the lifted sword slashing at his head. In trying to turn away he stumbled. He fell and there was one blinding stab of pain at the back of his neck.

CHAPTER ELEVEN

When Houston finally reached Gonzales on March 11, he found 374 men camped there under Moseley Baker. Although Baker and Houston had had their differences, they now buried their enmity.

'Any news from the Alamo?' Houston demanded, sliding from his horse.

Baker shook his head. 'I figure Fannin must have gone to help—'

A sudden wail of women from the town put a cold lump in Houston's throat. For he felt certain he knew the cause of the sounds of anguish. Two Mexicans, themselves fleeing Santa Anna, had roared into town, spreading the story of massacre at the Alamo. The widows of the Gonzales men who had gone to Travis' aid were weeping.

Knowing he had to go to extreme measures to keep his meager forces under control, Houston denounced the Mexicans as spies, sent by Santa Anna to put terror into Texas hearts. He ordered them arrested.

As soon as the protesting Mexicans were led away, Houston wrote Fannin, who was at Goliad with a sizable force.

Fannin, you will as soon as practicable, after the receipt of this order, fall back upon Guadalupe Victoria with your command and such artillery as can be brought with expedition. The remainder will be sunk in the river. You will take the necessary measures for the defence of Victoria and forward one third of your effective men to this point, and remain in command until further orders...

Desperate to whip some semblance of an army into shape before the Alamo disaster could be confirmed, Houston drilled his men day and night. However, Deaf Smith, the scout, arrived with three actual survivors, Mrs. A. M. Dickinson, her infant daughter, Angelina, and

142

Travis' negro servant.

Now there was no way Houston could discount the story as the work of Santa Anna spies. Here was the attractive widow of a Texas officer who had perished on the walls of the Alamo.

'Hit Santa Anna head on!' was the cry that went up from Houston's men.

But Houston, formidable in the twilight shadows that darkened the river at his back, raged at the men. Finally they fell silent.

'We're going to meet Fannin on the Colorado. That will give us a force of some size. Until then we retreat.'

'Retreat!' somebody shouted. 'Texans never retreat!'

Again Houston waved his large hands, silencing the angry murmur from his men. 'We had one massacre at the Alamo. Let's not have another!'

It was Houston's iron will that finally prevailed. Because they had to move swiftly to prevent encirclement by Santa Anna's men, Houston ordered the two cannon at Gonzales wheeled into the river and sunk.

They marched out. A rear guard in command of Deaf Smith would bring the refugees from Gonzales. As they moved out, the first hint of spring was in the air. All that black night the men marched, stumbling blindly in the deep sand, cursing Houston under their breath. For

143

they were now dismounted troops, not cavalry.

'What Texan can fight without a hoss under him?' one of them complained.

At dawn Houston called a halt and the exhausted troops sank to the ground and slept. The refugee train ground up. When the soldiers awakened, the women were cooking breakfast for them.

Deaf Smith got Houston aside. 'Some of the boys have deserted. They've gone to Goliad to join Fannin.'

Houston gave the scout a bitter look. 'They'll stir up Fannin and his men.' And he knew that Fannin had the best troops, far superior to the untrained rabble now under his own command.

To bear out Houston's prediction word came from Fannin: 'We will not retreat!'

'The fool!' Houston paced the camp, kicking gouts of sand with his great boots in anger. 'Will we never have even a semblance of discipline in this Texas army?'

When Houston and his men finally reached the Colorado River they found the bank lined with refugees. Houston rode among them, trying to quell the terror he saw in the eyes of the women and their children. Husbands and fathers were grimly determined to get their families to the other side of the river. The terrible news of massacre had been spread far and wide by those who had deserted and gone to join Fannin.

144

Houston wrote the president of the Republic, David G. Burnet: 'If only three hundred men remain on this side of the Brazos, I will die with them or conquer.'

Although some members of the government had fled when news of the Alamo reached them, a nucleus stood firm. There were those who claimed that with the six hundred men Houston had accumulated at the Colorado he had a sufficient force with which to meet Santa Anna.

'And risk defeat, which will mean the end of the rebellion!' Houston stormed. 'Probably the extermination of every Anglo-Saxon in Texas.'

Closing his mind to the dissenters, Houston moved down the river. Deaf Smith returned from a scouting mission with a Mexican prisoner. Under questioning by Houston, the Mexican revealed that General Sesma, with seven hundred men and two field pieces, was on forced march to annihilate the Texas forces. Other Mexican columns were also in the area.

Although some of his men showed panic, Houston held firm. In the distance smoke from Sesma's camp darkened the sky.

For nearly a week the two armies braced for battle with only a river between them. The only activity was sporadic firing between patrols.

On March 25, one of those who had deserted to join Fannin arrived at Houston's tent on a floundering mount. 'Fannin was defeated at Goliad!' the man announced.

145

Houston swore mightily. All along he had hoped Fannin would choose finally to obey his commander's orders.

When the news of the defeat spread across the camp, Houston drew his officers around him. Crowding his mind was the plight of Fannin and his men at Goliad. Houston had two courses open to him. He could hurl his meager force at General Sesma and risk defeat. With Fannin's crack troops out of the fighting there would be no chance for the rest of Texas if Houston's force met disaster.

'Load the wagons!' he ordered his officers, finally making up his mind. 'We retreat at sunset!'

A wave of anger swept the ranks. Some officers who had advocated engaging Sesma were on the verge of mutiny. But at last they grudgingly gave in to the order. Leaving fires to fool the Sesma scouts, they marched at first dark. All night they kept to a punishing pace.

After a few hours' sleep, they came to a great swamp on the banks of the Brazos. As if this alone wasn't enough to try the spirits of the weary men, torrential rains suddenly descended. In the confusion wagons were bogged down. Sometimes it took a double team of oxen to pull wheels free of the sucking gumbo.

Houston was everywhere, shouting encouragement to his men. 'Rains can't last forever!' he grinned. 'Not even in Texas!'

Bone-weary after the forced march, they were in no mood for humor. Those who had left families behind were apprehensive as to their fate.

Under the punishing elements the back of the army seemed about to break. Through it all Houston's mighty voice, roaring above the crash of the storm, beat at them incessantly. But even so, men began to desert, slipping away in the darkness.

But the grumbling of the men suddenly ceased, when above the howl of the storm they heard a woman's sharp cry for help.

Men turned toward the sound in the murky daylight, the wind and rain so strong in their faces it seemed to suck the breath from the lungs.

Far out in the flooded river they saw an overturned wagon. Clinging to the side were a woman and two small children. As the men stood rooted in the mud, reflexes dulled by fatigue, they saw Houston drive his horse into the river.

'As if we don't have troubles enough,' one of the officers wailed, 'now we lose our general.'

Kicking off his boots, Houston grabbed the tail of his horse, urged it unerringly toward the wagon, that had caught against an island of driftwood.

The woman, her long pale hair streaming

along the roiled, muddy surface of the river, a child under each arm, was pinned against the mass of driftwood. The wagon had now broken free and was tumbling in the current far downstream.

'Hang on!' Houston shouted.

A wave of muddied water struck him and he went under. The very force of the river caused him to lose his grip on the tail of his mount. Gasping, he struggled to the surface. The horse was gone.

'Save my children!' cried the woman, nearer now. 'Never mind me!'

Houston's powerful arms cut through the water like the blades of a steamer paddlewheel. Finally Houston got a hand on the woman's arm. She was in her early twenties, quite pretty. Her dress was torn and he could see the gleaming cone of a white breast.

With a cry of despair she tried to get him to take her children and ignore her.

'I'll save you all,' he announced, and despite the odds against him he believed that he could.

But as he clung to the mass of driftwood that had been captured and held by some underwater object, he felt it begin to disintegrate under pressure from the river. A faint hope burgeoned when he saw that his men on the shore had spliced ropes and tied a four-foot chunk of driftwood to one end.

Three times they flung the weighted rope into

the river, but each time it fell short.

'Try again!' he yelled.

But already the rope came sailing out to him. This time he got the length of driftwood firmly wedged under his arms.

With his toes hooked into the moving driftwood island, he took a child under each arm. 'Put your arms around my neck,' he ordered the woman. 'Hang on.'

Slowly, inexorably, the sweating men on the bank began to draw them toward shore. At last, buffeted by the roaring river, they reached solid footing. Immediately Houston called for a cloak. This he put around the woman's exposed shoulders.

A great cry swept the ranks, for the men viewed the rescue as a miracle. 'Houston! Houston! Houston!' was the roar that went up. It was followed by, 'Long live Texas!'

That night the adulation was extinguished by tragedy. A messenger arrived with news from Goliad. Fannin and his 390 men, prisoners of the Mexicans, had been executed. The atrocity had been perpetrated under specific orders from General Santa Anna. Only a few Texans had escaped through a swamp.

There had been wild panic in Texas before. Now it was increased tenfold when this grim news spread across the country. Burnet's government began to topple. There was an hysterical flight of refugees toward the Sabine.

All that lay between the terrified settlers and the onrushing legions of Santa Anna was Sam Houston's mud-splattered, disorderly mob.

However, Houston had one cause for an exultant shout. Two pieces of artillery, donated by the citizens of Cincinnati, arrived.

'We'll call them the "Twin Sisters,"' Houston declared. 'A pair of iron females who will chew up Santa Anna for breakfast.'

With his position strengthened by cannon, Houston went looking for Santa Anna. Finally, after they were on the march again, Deaf Smith located *El Presidente*.

'Santa Anna is camped at Rio San Jacinto,' Smith reported.

'It's the news I've been waiting for,' Houston announced to his officers. They had been moving along Buffalo Bayou and now he made preparations to cross that body of water.

'But it's impossible,' one of the officers pointed out. At this point the bayou was three hundred and fifty feet wide and fifteen feet deep. 'We have only one leaky boat.'

'We'll manage,' Houston snapped.

He ordered spliced ropes to be stretched from bank to bank. While swimmers accomplished this, Houston cut a pair of poles into oars for the boat.

Ignoring danger, Houston was the first man to make the perilous crossing in the tub of a boat, his mount swimming behind.

150

CHAPTER TWELVE

It was during the ferrying of his troops that Houston wrote what he considered might very well be his final word: 'This morning we are in preparation to meet Santa Anna. It is the only chance of saving Texas.'

There were numerous accidents on the makeshift ferry, men spilled into the water, horses lost. However, by sundown the last man was across. The sick had been left with the wagons on the far bank.

They ate cold beef in a muddy camp. The men were strangely silent after the ordeal of crossing, for to speak took energy and they had none to spare.

After only a short rest, they were marching through the night, feet sucking in the mud, the occasional whinny of a horse the only sound.

Deaf Smith, who had been on a scouting expedition, returned to say that so far Santa Anna had not reached Lynch's Ferry, which would be in his direct line of march to engage the Texas army. It had been Houston's strategy to get there first. It meant that by force-marching his men under impossible weather conditions Houston had won a battle without the firing of a shot.

The next day they captured a flatboat loaded

with supplies for the Mexican troops.

'Luck is smiling on us, boys,' Houston grinned, and for the first time in days they had flour for bread and sugar and salt.

For his strategic stand, Houston chose a camp in a live oak grove. A twenty-foot bank that descended gradually to the bayou's edge provided a natural breastworks. Before it the terrain was flat, partially screened by a narrow band of timber. At Houston's left the marshes of the San Jacinto made an enemy approach difficult from that side. His right flank was protected by swiftly flowing streams.

Finally Santa Anna's men appeared on the flats in front of Houston's position. The opening shot of the battle came from a brass Mexican twelve-pounder. As the shot went screaming overhead, Santa Anna tried to overwhelm the Texans by a mass assault. But when the Mexican troops charged toward the breastworks, the Twin Sisters belched smoke and broken horseshoes, and the Mexicans were laid low as if by a giant scythe.

After the Mexicans withdrew, the Texans awaited the order to charge. But Houston did not give it.

A mutinous rumble again began to spread through the ranks. Even Houston's officers questioned his judgment in not attacking immediately.

But Houston stood his ground. 'I've studied

the character of Santa Anna. He and his men have been primed for battle. When we don't attack there will come a let-down. In a period of hours the Mexicans will lose a lot of their drive.'

'You can't be sure.'

'I'm gambling that I'm right.' Houston considered this his war, and by God he was going to run it his way. He had been defied by the government, suffered mutiny and desertion, while the tragedies of the Alamo and Goliad only added to his handicaps.

'Remember that we're raw militia facing seasoned troops,' Houston cautioned his officers. 'We have an entrenched position. I will decide when we leave it.'

Houston called for his trusted Deaf Smith. 'I want you to choose a good man. Take axes. Go to Vince's Creek. Destroy the bridge there.'

Smith grinned. 'Looks like we're gonna fight after all, don't it, General?'

Houston considered the destruction of the bridge an important strategy. The bridge, eight miles to the north, was on the single road leading to the Brazos. Both Houston and Santa Anna had crossed it to reach their present positions, which were hemmed in by Buffalo Bayou and the San Jacinto.

Later that day Houston said to his officers, 'We're going to attack.'

The left flank he assigned to Colonel Sherman. Colonel Millard was in charge of the right wing. The center position was under command of Colonel Burleson. The Twin Sisters were to be under the charge of Major Hockley. The cavalry, under the command of Colonel Mirabeau Lamar, was formed on the extreme right.

Houston glanced at the sun. By his calculations it was four o'clock. Siesta time.

A stained black coat hung from Houston's tremendous shoulders. His breeches were torn, stuffed into the tops of boots that would have been shunned even by a river derelict. His only symbol of command was the sword secured to his waist by a thong of buckskin.

Mounted on his white horse, Houston led the cautious advance. Because of the intervening stands of timber, the Texans were not noticed by Santa Anna's troops. Then the one fife and drum with the Texas outfit began to play *Come to the Bower I Have Shaded for You*. And as an overtone to this the Twin Sisters, lumbering forward, spewed their broken horseshoes into the Mexican camp.

Standing in the stirrups, Houston admonished his men to wait until they were close enough to pick a target.

'Don't waste ammunition.'

He turned in the saddle as Deaf Smith came pounding up. 'Vince's bridge!' the scout shouted. 'We cut 'er down!'

Grinning, Houston shook his fist at the

Mexican camp. 'No retreat for them or us!' Turning in the saddle, he looked back at his men. 'Follow me, boys!' he cried. 'Remember the Alamo!'

'Remember the Alamo!' was the battle cry that surged from the Texans as they charged. And another voice added to the din: 'Remember Goliad!'

Disorganized by the shot pouring from the cannon, the stunned Mexicans milled about. Those taking siesta were jarred awake by the deadly metal flanges hurled into their midst.

As the Texans gathered momentum, Houston cried, 'Hold your fire!' when some of the overeager began shooting at the Mexicans who were now pouring toward the breastworks.

It was at point-blank range that the Texans unleashed their first volley. The hapless Mexicans, bewildered by the sudden attack, were cut down. Because of the close quarters, the Texans did no reloading. Eager hands grasped rifle barrels, swinging the heavy weapons as clubs. Skulls were crushed in memory of those who had died at the Alamo.

In the first volley from the Mexicans, who were falling back, Houston felt a crushing blow at his ankle. Reeling in the saddle, he managed to grasp the horn and steady himself.

A fleeing Mexican officer fired directly at the long-haired giant who loomed above. It was Houston's horse that took the bullet. With its front legs folding, the animal threw Houston over its head.

On his knees, Houston struggled up. A Mexican fired a rifle almost in his face. But Houston had flung himself forward, the length of his sword angled upward. Impaled by Houston's thrust, the *soldado* collapsed.

Ripping free his sword, Houston hobbled about, smashing at heads, yelling, 'Remember the Alamo!'

Another horse was brought up, for he could hardly stand now, so great was the pain of his wound. In the maelstrom his second horse was hit.

This time Houston had to be helped to his feet. Because the Mexicans were in flight, he yelled at his men, 'Boys, the battle's won. Pull back with your prisoners!'

But even his powerful voice failed to carry above the din. There was no stopping the frenzied Texans.

Some of the Mexicans, begging for mercy, screamed, 'Me no Alamo. Me no Alamo!' But whether they had participated in the massacre at the Alamo or not made no difference. When rifle stocks were shattered from pounding at skulls, the Texans used knives and their bare hands.

In their frantic efforts to escape, the Mexicans streamed down the Harrisburg road. But they soon found that Vince's bridge had been destroyed. The Mexican cavalry tried to swim their horses to safety but were shot out of the saddle.

The slaughter would have been complete had not Houston at last made himself heard. White flags were everywhere in evidence. 'They've surrendered, damn it!' he cried.

'Remember the Alamo!'

'This isn't the Alamo,' Houston countered, grinding his teeth at the pain. 'We're Texans, not butchers!'

Even though to Houston the battle had seemed to rage for hours, in reality it was slightly under twenty minutes from the time the first shot was fired until surrender.

Throughout the night the Texans celebrated: 'Sam Houston, hero of San Jacinto!' was the cry that rolled across the plain. They were proclaiming him now with as much fervor as they had once denounced him and flaunted his authority.

'I told you them Mexicans couldn't fight,' boasted a grimy Texas volunteer.

'Don't be fooled,' Houston snapped. 'It was surprise that gave us the advantage.'

In the morning the 630 Mexican dead were viewed by Houston. But there was no sign of Santa Anna. However, a prisoner was finally brought in, a man dressed as a common soldier but wearing fine linen and jeweled studs under his coat.

'I am Santa Anna. *El Presidente!* I demand treatment as a prisoner of war. I surrender to you.'

'You did not surrender,' Houston reminded him. He lay on a blanket, under a huge tree, surrounded by his officers. 'You were captured, fleeing the field of battle.'

Santa Anna drew himself up. He was not a tall man, but there was something commanding in his manner. 'I ask mercy for the vanquished.'

'How much mercy did you give the vanquished at the Alamo?' Houston demanded.

'I only observed the rules of warfare. I ordered surrender and they refused.'

'It was barbaric and you know it!'

'I was under instructions from my government.'

Despite the pain of his wound, Houston managed a harsh laugh. 'You are a dictator. There is no one to give you orders.' Houston settled back on his blanket, easing his bandaged ankle. 'What would you do under similar circumstances, if you captured a general who had ordered the massacre of your countrymen?'

'I demand to be treated as a prisoner,' Santa Anna said, losing color, 'according to my rank, which is the highest in Mexico.'

One of Houston's young officers thrust a coil of rope in Santa Anna's face. 'I claim Santa Anna should die—not as a soldier, but hanged as a common murderer.'

A shout went up at this. But if Houston heard he gave no sign. He was staring at the coil of rope and his mind went back to the days of Nacogdoches and the man Tweedy who had come to demand in effect that his murderer be hanged. Today was the first time since then that he had been faced with the prospect of hanging a man. He wondered what had ever happened to Jesse Summer. He thought of how much help Jesse could have been to him through all these turbulent weeks. Had Jesse Summer possessed an ounce of courage, Houston thought, he would have presented himself and joined the army, no matter how stormy their parting had been. He supposed Summer and Mike Reardon were back in New Orleans, Reardon seeing if he could empty the city of its liquor supply, Summer testing the patience of numerous husbands.

Surely they must have heard of his urgent need for trained men, his need of comrades he could trust. And they had not bothered to answer his call for recruits. The hell with them both!

Now Houston looked up into the dark, sweating face of his captive. 'What if I gave in to the wishes of my men and hanged you?'

'I would protest this barbarous action.'

'With a noose around your neck, you would be in no position to protest anything.'

As if Houston's words were a sign of

159

approval, the young officer flung the rope over a tree limb above *El Presidente's* head. 'We'll haul him up for you, General. Nice and easy so it'll give him time to remember the Alamo and Goliad while he strangles.'

Santa Anna stared at the noose and clenched his teeth.

Houston said, 'You are my personal prisoner. I alone will decide your fate. But at the moment you will issue an order to your next in command.'

'That is General Filisola,' Santa Anna said, a faint hope in his eyes.

'And how many men does he have?'

'Three thousand.'

Houston whistled softly under his breath, thinking it fortunate indeed that Filisola had not been able to come to Santa Anna's aid in time. Otherwise the odds against the ragtag Texas army would have been overwhelming.

'You will issue a written order to General Filisola,' Houston snapped. 'He is to take his men out of Texas.'

'If I do this are you prepared to guarantee my safety?'

Houston pointed at the noose dangling above Santa Anna's head. 'You have no choice but to obey.'

Swallowing, Santa Anna took pen and paper handed him by one of the officers. '... I have agreed with General Houston for an armistice, until matters can be so regulated that the war shall cease forever.'

CHAPTER THIRTEEN

Again Houston was given no thanks for his herculean efforts. When Santa Anna's order to Filisola had been dispatched, Houston sent couriers to locate President Burnet and his faltering government. He soon learned they had taken refuge on Galveston Island.

When the president and his staff finally appeared at the San Jacinto battleground, they seemed to think they had won the war unaided. None of them tried to hide the enmity they felt toward Sam Houston.

To Major Hockley Houston said bitterly, 'They wanted a victory. I gave them one. Why do they hate me so?'

'Because they know they failed you.'

Due to the growing seriousness of his wound, Houston asked for a leave to go to New Orleans for treatment. Without funds, Houston was further humiliated by his own government when they did not even offer to pay for his passage. However, the captain of the schooner said it was an honor to have so heroic a figure aboard. Houston could pay for the passage later.

Despite his fever, Houston felt a lift of spirits when the schooner finally docked in New Orleans and on the levee he saw a huge throng shouting his name.

'The hero of San Jacinto!' they cried. 'He defeated the Mexicans!'

The following day he underwent surgery and twenty-two pieces of bone were removed from the shattered ankle.

As he recuperated at the home of friends, Houston received reports from Texas. Mirabeau B. Lamar had taken over the army and took it upon himself to stump the country, inflaming the populace against Santa Anna. 'He's a murderer, not a prisoner of war!' Lamar shouted. 'Just because Houston wants to coddle him is no reason we should.'

Lamar was openly heading the anti-Houston movement in Texas. Houston, sick as he was, penned a note, begging the government to consider the position of Santa Anna.

. . . Santa Anna is a vital asset to Texas, not a liability. Kill him and we will permanently isolate Mexico. We have to live on the border of that country for the life of our Republic. God grant that it may be long.

Houston also heard that in Mexico the news of the defeat at San Jacinto had been received as a great shock. But the Mexicans apparently were in no mood for revenge.

In New Orleans Houston asked one of his visitors if he had ever heard of Jesse Summer. 'He fought a duel here some years ago.'

The visitor chuckled. 'Yes, I remember him well.'

'Do you know if he still lives in this city?'

'Living here?' the man asked in some surprise. 'Why, Houston, he's been fighting for you. Didn't you know?'

Houston looked bewildered. 'I'm afraid not.'

'My brother was with Bowie during the siege of Bexar. He wrote that Summer and that friend of his, Reardon, were both there.'

'I'll be damned.'

'Summer was later with Fannin at Goliad.'

'The hell you say.'

'He was one of the handful of Texans who managed to escape through the swamps and avoid execution.'

Houston looked grim. 'There are many things, it seems, that I didn't know.'

'He's some sort of hero among his friends. My brother speaks very highly of him.'

'Old Jesse a hero!' Throwing back his head, Houston roared with laughter.

It was while his ankle healed that he met Margaret Lea, one of those who had been on the levee when he arrived from Texas. The large violet eyes of this dark-haired girl were filled with compassion when she hesitantly entered the garden where he was daily taking the sun at the home of a friend.

Although he insisted he could take care of himself, she declared she would help nurse him and there was no use arguing the matter. It wasn't every day a girl got to meet a hero.

When he was able to hobble about on crutches, she accompanied him. For the first time in months he felt a sense of peace in the presence of this girl. They would walk along the levee and watch the steamers and see the great flocks of birds winging under the cotton-white clouds.

He told her of his days in Washington, of his friendship with Andrew Jackson, of his hopes for Texas.

'I think it's shameful the way they've treated you in Texas,' Margaret cried. 'President Burnet's government is unstable, the country is in panic and they insult and degrade the one man who could help them—you.'

On this day Houston and Margaret were being driven in a carriage along the canals. Houston said bitterly, 'I'm the one person Texas doesn't need.'

'If they only knew you as you really are.'

He gave her a tired smile. 'What do *you* know about me?'

'You have always been a hero in my eyes. I've read about you. My mother has spoken of you often. You're no stranger to me.'

164

'I am very humble in your presence,' he said softly.

At that moment the carriage wheels hit a rut, and Houston was jolted against Margaret. He found her lips with his. She did not turn away. And instantly, when her arms tightened about his neck, he knew there must have been some divine reason for his escaping with his life, even by such a slim margin—to find this dark-haired girl.

'You should go back to Texas and fight for what you believe to be right,' Margaret said, flushing a little as she adjusted her bonnet.

The lines in Houston's face were deeper now since the ordeal of the retreat and the battle at San Jacinto. 'I wonder if they would welcome me,' he said somberly, remembering past insults, his wounded pride.

'Sam, I have a surprise for you.' Her eyes were shining.

'What sort of surprise?'

'You'll see.'

Leaning forward, she told the coachman to drive to her house. There in the parlor, with the sun streaming through rose-tinted, leaded, windows, Houston saw a group of Texans waiting for him. With them was Jesse Summer.

Houston, leaning on his crutch, shouted, 'Jesse!'

Summer, looking older, his face drawn

165

although still handsome, hurried forward. They shook hands.

'We parted in bitterness,' Houston said quietly.

'I was to blame, not you.'

'They tell me you've been fighting for Texas, Jesse.'

'Some.' Jesse Summer wore broadcloth, a little shiny and worn at the cuffs. But his shirt was spotless, his boots highly polished. There seemed to be a new calmness about the man, Houston thought, a new determination to make something of his life.

'Have you seen Mike Reardon?' Houston asked.

Summer looked away. 'We had a fight at Bexar. It was a stupid thing, really. One of the few times in my life I was gallant. I tried to save a girl who was already doomed.' He shrugged. 'But now there are more pressing matters. Sam, we want you to run for president.'

Houston's mouth fell open. 'You're joking.'

'We were never more serious,' one of the others spoke up. 'We think you can win the election.'

'We *know* you can win,' Summer cut in. 'There isn't time to mull this over, Sam. We want you to come back with us and accept the nomination.'

Houston stared at the men. 'It would mean running against Stephen Austin. That I don't like.'

166

'Austin can't win against Smith. We need a strong government. Without it Texas is doomed.'

Standing at the back of the room was Margaret Lea, her eyes shining with pride. When Houston looked at her questioningly, she nodded. Houston turned to the men. 'I'll go on one condition. When I return to Texas we'll see how the people react.'

'They'll react favorably,' Jesse Summer smiled.

*   *   *

True of Summer's prediction, Houston's victory was substantial. He received, 5,119 votes to 743 for Smith and 587 for Austin.

The only mistake, Houston felt, was the selection of Mirabeau Lamar as vice-president. President Burnet, so anxious to throw down the burden of the presidency, resigned before the inauguration.

Houston took office in October, 1836. In a large barn-like structure in Columbia, Texas, Houston took the oath of office, standing before a blanket-covered table.

As his first act as president, he unbuckled the sword he had carried at San Jacinto and said to Congress, 'It now . . . becomes my duty to make a presentation of this sword—this emblem of my past office.' As the assemblage looked on he

167

choked up momentarily. Then he firmly clenched the sword in both hands as if with a farewell grasp. 'I have worn it with some humble pretensions in defence of my country ... Should my country call ... I expect to resume it.'

For the next several days he was busy with appointments, issuing instructions, approving some measures, rejecting others. The previous administration had been in such chaos it took three secretaries to transcribe his notes pertaining to unfinished business. Congress was in a continual state of awe of this man while the cabinet was stunned by the swiftly moving events set in motion by Houston.

Austin was made Secretary of State. Although crushed by his overwhelming defeat at the polls, Austin salvaged some measure of pride in the generous appointment by Houston.

Despite Houston's sweeping victory in the election, there were still those who thought him daft not to execute Santa Anna.

One day as he was out walking, he was accosted by Colonel Reece Stapleton, a pompous former slaveholder from Mobile. 'Mr. President,' the colonel said thinly, 'I represent a group who wish to see Santa Anna executed at the first possible moment.'

'I have no use for Santa Anna. Neither do a majority of Mexican people,' Houston told him. 'But if Santa Anna is executed, it will give them

168

a bond, and a reason to stir up more trouble for us. Trouble we can't afford while we are trying to found a republic.'

At that moment a New Orleans carriage, incongruous on this frontier street, appeared. A tall, black-haired woman in her late twenties leaned out. 'I have finished my shopping,' she said to the colonel.

Stapleton did not look around at his attractive wife. He was glaring at Houston. 'One moment, Nona. Mr. President, you are not without enemies in Texas.'

'I am used to enemies.'

Stapleton swore under his breath and stepped to the carriage. 'Mark my words. Spare Santa Anna and you'll be in for trouble.' He shook his fist.

Houston, who had removed his hat in the presence of the colonel's wife, now set it firmly on his head. 'Don't threaten me, Colonel,' he said coldly. 'Good day, Mrs. Stapleton.'

Sometime later he encountered Jesse Summer, who had put on weight and looked almost as young as he had back in Nacogdoches. Houston told of his encounter with the colonel.

'He seeks to stir up trouble for your administration,' Summer said. 'Then his own crowd can take over. I understand he's dickering for thousands of acres of swampland which he intends to sell to unsuspecting

169

Northerners.'

'Not while I'm president.'

'That's just the idea, Sam. To get you out of office so he and his cronies can shear the sheep, so to speak.'

'I'll have him thrown out of the army.'

'And that would give your esteemed vice-president, Lamar, an excuse to kick up a fuss.'

Houston smiled. 'I gave you a job. To keep your ear to the ground. I'd say you're doing remarkably well.'

Summer's gaze darkened. 'It's the colonel's wife I feel sorry for. I understand that on occasion he's beaten her.'

'She seems like a spirited woman. The beatings I doubt very much.'

'Any man who would strike a woman,' Jesse Summer said heatedly, 'deserves a caning.'

Houston continued to denounce those who clamored for the death of *El Presidente*. In his large voice he cried that Santa Anna should be sent to Washington for a visit with Jackson. And to make sure that Santa Anna started the journey without mishap, Houston saw him off.

Finances for the new republic were the pressing need for the moment. 'We need five million dollars,' Houston told Congress, and demanded authorization of a bond issue for that amount. Agents were sent to Washington to negotiate for a loan.

Shortly after Christmas Stephen Austin died. Bowed with grief at the death of this man who almost single-handedly was responsible for the initial colonization of Texas, Houston dictated an announcement: 'The father of Texas is no more. The first pioneer of the wilderness has departed.'

Later, Houston received a new blow. One of his representatives in Washington wrote: 'The panic which has followed Van Buren's inauguration has killed all chances of obtaining the five million dollar loan which was being negotiated.'

Houston scowled blackly at the barren wall across the office. 'Why must a man suffer such burdens?' he said aloud. In contrast the pleasant days of his recuperation in New Orleans, in the company of Margaret Lea, crossed his mind. To take his mind off his problems of government he wrote her a long letter.

One day Jesse Summer came to Houston, looking worried. 'Did you ever know a man named Bowheen? Rufe Bowheen?'

Houston, who had been signing documents, put down his pen. 'The name means nothing to me.'

Summer spread the tails of his dark coat and sat on the edge of Houston's desk. 'I was in Bexar recently. I overheard this Bowheen say that if it was ever within his power he'd see you destroyed. Or any of your friends destroyed.'

'I'm not surprised. My enemies are like the fleas that pester an old dog.'

'This Bowheen seems unusually vehement. From what I could gather his grudge against you goes back many years.'

Still the name meant nothing to Houston. He asked Summer to describe the man.

'One outstanding feature about the man you'd never forget. He has a nose, not only broken, but smashed almost flat against his face.'

'Doesn't sound like anyone I ever knew.' Houston picked up his pen, toyed with it for a moment. 'Jesse, there's a rumor that you and Nona Stapleton—'

Jesse Summer's handsome face lost color. 'I know what you're thinking. But it isn't the same—'

'For God's sake stay away from Stapleton's wife. He's a hot-headed fool. It could mean your death.'

'The man is a beast. She's shown me her black and blue marks.'

Houston settled back in his chair, regarding the younger man narrowly. 'Jesse, you have the heart of a pirate. Always wanting something possessed by another.'

'The remark may have been deserved in the past. But this time it is love. True love.'

'And she returns this fervor?' Houston asked skeptically.

'It means giving up a life of ease. But she'll divorce Stapleton and marry me.'

'Then if you've reached an agreement, have the woman leave Texas. Let her go somewhere else and get her divorce. Although I warn you divorcing a colonel won't be easy. She'll have to have proof.'

'Never fear.' Summer smiled.

'I hope for your sake things work out.'

'This is a matter of honor, Sam. I have sworn not to touch her again until she is my wife.'

'This matter of restraint,' Houston said quietly, 'is something new for you, Jesse. But I wish you well.'

'My affairs won't be an added stone around your neck.'

Houston shrugged, then said seriously, 'When you were in Bexar did you see Mike Reardon by any chance?'

'I went to the place where we had the fight. The girl who was the cause of it—' Summer gave a sour smile—'is now quite a professional. Nobody's seen Mike.'

'Probably lying in some unmarked grave,' Houston said somberly. 'But I hope not.'

Jesse Summer took his leave of the president and hurried out. The sun beat unmercifully on the back of his neck. How could he get in touch with Nona? Of course, he could try and find Moffat, the Stapleton coachman, in one of the taverns and give him a message. But this he hated to do. He didn't put quite as much trust in the man as Nona did.

At their last meeting he had gallantly suggested they not see each other again until matters were legally straightened out between her and the colonel.

He waited in a tavern, drinking sparingly. At last he was rewarded by the sight of her tall figure through the window. She was holding her skirts above the dust which closed over her shoes as she crossed the street. Paying for his drinks, Summer hurried out.

As he overtook her he saw the knot of black hair at the back of the creamy neck. Her whole body seemed to struggle sensually against the dress of green silk.

'Nona,' he said, as he caught up, not looking at her. 'I must see you. The rock.' This had been their rendezvous in their past, more indiscreet meetings.

'In an hour,' she whispered, and continued on to her house at the far end of town.

Getting his horse, Summer rode leisurely out of town to the north, then circled south, in case the colonel or any of his friends might become suspicious. Despite his beastly conduct toward his wife, the colonel was a popular figure.

In the center of an oak grove, not far from a wagon road, was a fair-sized cave at the base of a rock spire. Tethering his horse, Summer

174

waited. He had about given her up when he heard the sounds of a carriage. The Stapleton carriage driven by Moffat, a wiry, red-faced man, came up through the trees.

Summer kept out of sight until she alighted and Moffat, without looking around, drove back toward the town. Only then did Summer step into view.

'Of all the fool things,' he snapped. 'To let Moffat bring you here—'

'I love you when you're angry,' she smiled, hurrying to him. 'Next thing I know you'll beat me as Reece does.'

'Your husband's foul ways are nothing to joke about.'

She lowered her gaze. 'I know. I'm sorry.'

He pointed out that on their previous meetings she had come alone, riding her mare sidesaddle. 'But today—'

'Reece bruised me last night,' she whispered and gingerly rubbed herself. 'I could hardly sit in the carriage without discomfort, let alone a jolting saddle.'

'My poor darling.' He caught her in his arms. Her lips were moist. They broke apart. 'What if Moffat tells the colonel?'

'I trust Moffat implicitly. He'll return for me in an hour.'

'You know it's madness to trust him.'

'Talk is a waste,' she said huskily. 'We don't have much time.'

In the cave he spread his coat for her and eased her down on it. Dark eyes brooding, she stared out at the forest and the wagon tracks through the trees.

He sank down beside her. 'We've got to talk rationally.' But his voice faltered as he tried mightily to stem the desire the nearness of this fabulous woman stirred in him. 'I had a talk with Houston. He knows about us.'

'Don't tell me you're afraid of my husband?'

'No, but I must protect the president as well as you. I'm Houston's friend. Any scandal would give the president's enemies—'

A vein like a blue thread against ivory began to throb in her temple. 'Is that the only reason you asked me here? To talk about Houston.'

He started to tell her the truth, but under the circumstances it seemed fatuous with this woman beside him, her breasts thrusting sharply against the green dress. 'I want you to go to New Orleans. Divorce the colonel. God knows you have cause.'

'He treated me brutally last night, Jesse.'

'For what reason this time?' Summer demanded.

'He needs no reason. Somehow using his hands on me inflames him. He treats me as a naughty child who periodically needs discipline.'

'Why didn't you leave him years ago!'

'Jesse, I was only fourteen when we married.

176

I've never known anyone but Reece Stapleton.'
'Obviously he should be chained up in a madhouse.' He caught her warm hands. 'It's all the more reason for you to leave. Before he does something worse to you.'

She lay back on his cloak, her narrowed eyes bright through dark lashes. 'You are my only comfort. Later we can talk about divorce and such matters.'

The restraint he had mentioned to Houston seemed to flee. He leaned against her. Her lips formed soundless words as she pressed them against his mouth. Then he felt a sharp needle-like pain at his lip and the taste of his own blood.

'Jesse, Jesse,' she moaned, and her shaking fingers moved to the buttons of her dress.

Desperate with urgency now, he helped her, cursing the fact that women seemed to find it fashionable to be so completely enveloped in cotton and silks and whalebone.

At last, their garments in a common pile in the cave, she turned over on her stomach. 'Look what he did to me last night.'

For a moment his blood cooled in anger at sight of an ugly purple bruise the size of a human hand.

But she quickly turned on her back, pulling him down. 'You are my one true love,' she said hoarsely. And as she took him, her back arched, her naked flesh pressed close, there was a looseness about her mouth. 'Jesse, don't make me wait again—'

'The ground must hurt you,' he said in one last moment of compassion.

'Pain is love,' she breathed. 'Love is pain.' But her words were lost in the roaring sound that spilled through his brain as their bodies joined and he possessed her fully and completely.

Later a faint hum of warning penetrated his consciousness. Alarmed, he tore himself free of her and saw three pairs of legs at the cave mouth.

As he came up, something smashed him in the head. He dropped like a stone. But the blow had only paralyzed him, leaving a thread of consciousness.

As if from a great distance he heard Nona scream. Three renegades had come upon them and would now turn rapist, was the thought that streaked across his mind.

Curled up half in the cave, half out, his smoky vision cleared. He could see the blue dome of sky above the trees. He found he could turn his head. He saw Nona, her naked breasts heaving, her long black hair tangled about her shoulders. Holding her by the wrists were the coachman, Moffat, and the handy man from the Stapleton place. Colonel Reece Stapleton, wearing a plum-colored coat, was facing Nona.

'Reece, let me put on my clothes!' Nona screamed.

'You are a woman without shame.' The colonel turned to his two men. 'Don't let her get away. But don't look at her, understand? When it's over, I may take her down to the road and tie her to a tree and let all who pass witness her shame.'

'You wouldn't dare!' she cried, and tried to struggle but the two men, their eyes averted as the colonel had ordered, did not lose their grip on her wrists.

'But first there is other business,' the colonel went on. Turning, he looked at Summer, lying at the mouth of the cave. He bared his large, blunt teeth in a chilling smile. The colonel pointed at his wife. 'Look at her, Summer. Look long and remember.'

'You woman-beater!' Summer cried, and felt a return of energy to the previously paralyzed muscles.

Stapleton said, 'It is the last time in your life you will ever look upon a woman with desire.' He snapped a hand under the plum-colored coat. 'I didn't have much use for the late Jim Bowie. But he did fashion a knife of some merit.'

As Stapleton advanced, Jesse Summer watched the knife blade glinting in the sunlight. There was a twitching coldness at the back of Summer's neck.

The colonel halted a few feet away. 'Eunuch I

179

believe is the word,' Stapleton snapped and came forward, bending low, the knife held like a sword.

Nona Stapleton screamed, 'Reece, for God's sake—'

With the colonel upon him, Summer suddenly flung out a hand. He caught the man by an ankle and yanked with all the power of his arm and shoulder. The colonel's feet shot out from under him. The Bowie knife clattered against the cave wall as the colonel came down hard on his back.

Lurching to his feet, Summer snatched up the knife. 'Let her go!' he ordered the pair who held Nona. They took one look at the knife and obeyed. 'Turn your backs on her.' And when this was done, he told her to get dressed.

As if suddenly overcome with modesty she hurried to the cave, hunched over, trying to hide herself with hands and forearms.

Summer searched the stunned colonel, found a Derringer and flung it into the trees.

When Nona was dressed, Summer quickly put on his own clothes, keeping an eye on the pair who stood rigidly across the clearing, their backs turned.

The colonel sat up. He put a hand to the back of his head that had struck a stone when he fell. There was a trace of blood on his fingertips.

Summer said, 'Mrs. Stapleton is going to divorce you.'

180

Nona bit her lip. 'No, Jesse, no. Don't say such a thing!'

'There's no reason for you to fear him now.'

Stapleton got slowly to his feet, felt for his Derringer, then let his hand drop. 'A duel should settle the ownership of my wife,' he said.

Nona went pale. 'Reece, I am not a slave to be sold!'

The colonel ignored her. 'A duel with pistols, Summer. Unless you are a coward of the worst sort, I expect you on this spot tomorrow at dawn. Is that agreed?'

'Agreed,' Summer said stiffly.

'Nona,' Stapleton told his wife, 'the carriage is back in the trees. Moffat will drive you home, then come back for me and the hired man. You stay in your room, I'll stay in mine until this thing is settled.'

Head down, Nona was moving toward the carriage, and when Summer protested, she said, 'I'll be all right.'

'You could spend the night with friends,' Summer urged.

'No, I'll go to the house.'

When the carriage had gone, Summer got his horse. 'Until dawn,' he told the colonel.

'A suggestion,' smiled Colonel Stapleton. 'Make your will.'

★   ★   ★

At dawn, with the promise of the day's heat already over the land, five men gathered in the clearing before the cave. In the party were Stapleton and his second. For his second Summer had chosen a man named Grimes. The fifth member of the party was Dr. Barnes, the referee and surgeon.

'You will take ten paces, gentlemen,' said the doctor as he handed them identical pistols. 'At my count of ten you will turn and fire at will.'

Summer and the colonel approached each other, their features taut. There was a beading of perspiration on the colonel's forehead.

He leaned forward and whispered, 'You will find that adversity increases my wife's passion. If you live, that is. Which I doubt.'

Contemptuously the colonel turned his back. Dr. Barnes began the count.

As he stepped away, Jesse felt a coldness in the pit of his stomach. The count reached five, six—

God, he thought, *what if I lose? What will happen to Nona?*

'Seven—eight—nine—'

At the count of ten, Summer turned, his pistol cocked. But even before he swung completely around, he saw that Stapleton had stolen a second or two. The colonel was already firing. With the wicked snarl of the colonel's bullet going past his ear, Summer let the hammer of his pistol fall.

Stapleton's mouth snapped open. He hunched forward, weaved, and then collapsed. As the two seconds stood rigid, Dr. Barnes, a stout man with bushy side whiskers, knelt beside Stapleton. In a moment he rose and removed his hat.

'Gentlemen, Colonel Stapleton is dead.'

Feeling a little sick, Jesse Summer walked unsteadily to his horse. Later, with a drink to settle his stomach, Summer rode along the alley past Brown's Tavern, pulling up when he heard harsh voices.

He heard Dr. Barnes saying, 'Gentlemen, it was honorably done. It was a duel.'

'The hell with that!' a man shouted. 'The colonel was our friend. Summer is going to pay for this foul deed!'

Backing his horse to the rear of the tavern, Summer considered his position. Behind him the sound of an angry crowd increased. He rode quickly to the Stapleton house south of town.

He wanted to see Nona and explain how it had happened. He had planned to delay their meeting to give her time to compose herself. But now they had to flee.

However, it was Moffat, the coachman, who met him on the veranda. 'The Missus, she knows about the colonel,' Moffat said. 'She's sort of broke up.' The coachman lowered his voice. 'If I was you, Summer, I'd get the hell out of this town. You won't be alive to see another sun if you don't. The colonel's friends—'

'Tell Mrs. Stapleton that I will communicate with her.'

Even though to run this way seemed cowardly, he put spurs to his horse. There were others involved beside himself. Nona and Sam Houston. He would locate and then send for her. And he would write Sam and try to make him understand.

He turned his horse and looked back at the big house with its curtained windows. Lifting his hat, he waved, hoping she would see him. He knew in his heart that she would wait for him always.

As he rode he searched his consciousness and could find no way to blame himself for what had happened. It was the colonel's mistreatment of Nona that had brought them together. Small loss to the world, Summer told himself, that such a man with a twisted mind now lay dead.

CHAPTER FOURTEEN

When Houston learned that Colonel Stapleton had been killed by Summer, he slammed a fist on top of his desk. 'Damn Jesse Summer. What have I ever done to deserve a friend like him?'

184

And because he could not get Summer out of his mind, he sat at his desk in the twilight, with a drink in his hand. He thought of the old days when Reardon and Summer had helped him fight his way to the packet tied up at the Nashville dock.

As he stared at the desk a name suddenly flashed into his consciousness. *Bowheen!* The name Jesse Summer had mentioned. A man who intensely hated Sam Houston. A man with a nose not only broken but smashed against his face.

Of course. Rufe Bowheen. It was all sweeping back to him now—the humiliation he had suffered at the tavern near Fort Gibson when he had drunkenly tried to ward off the fists of a sober young giant...

*　　　*　　　*

Due to Houston's economic policies, the government at last began to prosper and even though Mexico refused to recognize Texas' independence a flourishing trade was built between the two countries.

In honor of the president the capital was moved from Columbia to a town named for him. Although he was flattered by having his headquarters in Houston, he was soon to realize a new harassment.

'Will the burdens never cease?' he wrote to

Margaret Lea, who was now living in Alabama with her mother.

My own vice-president is busy stirring up all the old and ugly stories about me. I hope you will discount most of what you hear. Although I admit a portion is the truth. But can't a man escape his past? What has happened to The Golden Rule? Or is it only something that we cherish briefly on a churchgoing Sunday morning.

Because of the antagonism of Vice-President Lamar, a new opposition developed against Houston. Behind his back men began to snicker as they had in the past. 'So he was the Big Drunk, christened so by his own Cherokees?'

Pamphlets were printed, distorting his role in the victory of San Jacinto. His pride was severely shaken when one of the pamphlets featured a cartoon showing him lounging under a tree while his troops did the fighting.

He wrote Margaret Lea:

It will soon be over, thank God. A constitutional provision bars me from serving a second consecutive term. I said once that I wash my hands of them. I do so again. You were wrong, Margaret, in saying the people of Texas wanted me.

Without Houston's name in nomination Mirabeau Lamar became president. One of Lamar's first acts was a direct slap at Houston. He caused the capital to be moved from the town Houston to Austin.

When Houston learned that Lamar intended a harsher policy toward the Indians, he said, 'Lamar turns his venom on the Cherokees. He calls them "Houston's pet Indians." There will be Indian trouble, mark me on that.'

In order to stave off what he felt to be disaster, Houston donned his old buckskins and rode out to the Indian country and pleaded with the chiefs to ignore Lamar.

But they showed him an order sent by the Texas government. It demanded that the Indians surrender their arms and leave the country.

'This we will never do!' the chiefs told Houston.

And when Houston rode to Austin and tried to point out the folly of the program, one of President Lamar's aides said, 'Texas is for Texans, not for Indians. A force of seven hundred Texans is on the march. This will be a campaign of extermination.'

'It's barbaric!' Houston cried, but he was powerless to halt the great battle shaping up. On July 14, 1839, the Texans overwhelmed a large force of Indians, breaking the power of the redman.

187

During these trying times Houston received a letter from Jesse Summer. It was very brief:

I am truly sorry that it has been my misfortune to add to your burdens. The Widow Stapleton has joined me at long last. I suppose that to ask for your blessing would be an imposition. Your friend, Jesse.

After a lucky win at cards, Summer had been able to ranch in a small way just across the border in Mexico. Because he had a certain air about him and spoke pure Spanish, he passed himself off to the natives as Castilian. They tolerated not only him but also his dolt of a hired man, a former teamster named Slagg. Here Summer was known as Señor Alvarez.

For weeks Summer had looked forward to Nona's arrival. When the great day finally came he was disappointed. She seemed distant and her embrace lacked the old fervor. In the small stone house where they lived, she drank too much wine and he would catch her staring at him strangely.

Although he didn't like her to drink so much, he decided to say nothing for the time being. Likely she was still in a state of shock at the death of the colonel. She hadn't had an easy time of it.

One day after he had been practicing marksmanship with his new five-shot revolver in the draw beyond Slagg's cabin, he came home to find her quite drunk.

'If you don't want me to drink,' she said, holding a glass of wine in her hand, 'why don't you beat me?'

'I remember you saying once that love is pain,' he told her thinly. 'It isn't to me.'

When he sat down at his desk in a corner of the room, she swayed over to him and said, 'You're a hard man to anger, Jesse!' Then she emptied the glass of wine into his lap.

When he just sat there, glaring up at her, she suddenly flung herself across his lap, face down, her long black hair touching the floor. 'I'm a naughty child,' she said hoarsely. 'I should be punished.'

'I find a faint disgust in this,' he snapped, and pushed her off his lap. After changing his wine-soaked trousers, he rode to the village. At the *cantina* over a drink he tried to puzzle out her strange behavior. It wasn't the first time she had goaded him almost beyond endurance. The feeling grew in him that her strange desires were somehow mixed up with intense hatred for him. But why? The answer eluded him.

When he returned he found her waiting for him. She was barefoot. With an enigmatic smile on her lips, she unbuttoned her dress and let it fall to her feet. He saw with some surprise that she wore nothing else.

'Jesse,' she said sweetly, 'when you go down

to your hired man's cabin, will you get my underclothes? I forgot to bring them home.'

He felt his face turn to ice under her taunting gaze. 'Do I understand,' he said in a voice he did not recognize as his own, 'that you have been with that half-wit Slagg?'

'He's a bruising lover.' She thrust out her arms suddenly so he could see the ugly black and blue marks.

Trembling, Summer lifted a fist, then lowered it. 'So this is retribution ... for all the dark deeds of my life.'

'Still there is no fight in you, Jesse, no anger!'

'Is that why you came to me in the first place? To infuriate the colonel so he would beat you?'

She leaned forward, spitting at him now, the handsome face contorted. 'I found pleasure in my affair with you. I enjoyed showing you my bruises, and this in turn would enrage you.'

'You're drunk and disgusting!'

'But then you had to kill my husband!'

'It was a duel, or have you forgotten?'

'I was the wife of a colonel. But since he died I have been shunned. That is why I waited so long to come to you. I weighed two possibilities: to go away and change my name and begin life anew—or to make you pay for destroying my life.'

'And so you have your revenge.' Summer stiffened his shoulders under his coat. 'By going to Slagg.'

'I have my revenge in other ways. Good-by, Jesse.' Picking up the dress, she walked majestically into the bedroom and bolted the door.

Summer pushed the five-shot revolver under his coat and walked down to Slagg's cabin. The place was empty. He saw the twisted blankets on a cot. On a chair were the garments Nona had mentioned.

Stepping outside, he glanced at the corral. Slagg's horse was gone.

As he started for the house four Mexicans suddenly stepped from behind a shed. Three were *soldados*. The fourth was tall, slender. They all carried rifles. Grinning, the tall one gave a little bow.

'The *Señora* said we would find you here. I am of the Mexican army. Captain Romero at your service.'

Summer froze. 'Just what do you want?'

'The *Señora* says you participated in the siege at Bexar. So that makes you a rebel from Texas.'

'The siege of Bexar is past history.'

Romero shook his head. 'Orders issued at the time by *El Presidente* were to the effect that all rebels are to be executed. My brother lost his life at Bexar. Therefore, I shall hang you, *Señor*.'

Summer thought swiftly. 'No, not that, *Señor!*'

The three Mexican soldiers leaned on their rifles, laughing. To see this *Americano* beg for his life was highly amusing. Summer was on his knees, pleading.

Captain Romero shared their mirth, but in a more restrained manner. 'The *Señora* must hate you, *Señor*. She communicated with me some days ago. We wait for her signal today.'

'What signal?'

'She says when you go down to this shack it is time to strike. That you will be unarmed. Now we hang you.'

Jesse Summer, on his knees, wondered then if Nona had really spent any time with Slagg—or whether she had lied, knowing he would go to the shack to shoot Slagg, knowing he wouldn't go unarmed. Did she arrange for this also to be a duel to the death? With the odds four to one?

'Mercy, *Señor*!' Summer cried and swiftly drew his pistol from beneath the coat. He shot Captain Romero in the stomach. As the captain pitched forward, Summer fired again, before the startled *soldados* could line their rifles. One of them fell against the shed with a shattered arm. The other two fled down a draw. Then Summer was riding swiftly for the Texas border, turning his back on the Widow Stapleton for all time.

192

CHAPTER FIFTEEN

True to Sam Houston's predictions, the Indian trouble grew worse and Lamar's government renched the verge of complete collapse. A new danger threatened. Because of Lamar's policies the Republic came dangerously close to war with Mexico.

A harassed Congress, after denouncing the administration as a miserable failure, prepared to adjourn *sine die*. But storming into the hall, Houston reproached them. 'Have you no shame?' he cried. 'Continue the government. Do not let it die!'

News that it was Houston's oratory, his personality, that had willed Congress to stay in session swept Texas. Once again, in a time of trouble, the people turned to Houston. He was hailed as the man who had saved the Republic.

But he did not stay to hear their plaudits. In Alabama, Houston took Margaret Lea as his bride. Attired in finery that would put to shame his shabby buckskins, or even the old dress uniform of San Jacinto, Houston knew the greatest triumph of his life.

A radiant Margaret, her violet eyes filled with the love she held for this giant of a frontiersman, whispered, 'I am the happiest woman in the world.'

In the room they shared he took her in his arms. 'There are no heights I cannot reach.' And he vowed to close his mind to the past for all time.

★　　★　　★

Because Houston had stepped in to force the government of Lamar to continue, instead of abandoning the Republic to anarchy, he was praised on every side.

'Forgive us, Sam, for the things we've done to you,' was the cry that went up.

With marriage as a steadying influence, Houston decided to again seek the presidency. And when the ballots were counted, Houston discovered he had been overwhelmingly elected. But his joy was short-lived. For when he took office in 1841 he found chaos.

In his inaugural message he berated his constituents, 'We are not only without money, but without credit. And for want of punctuality, without character.'

In the weeks that followed, Houston was seldom without pressure. Santa Anna had again come to power in Mexico, and once more there were skirmishes between the forces of both countries.

'This is my payment for saving him from execution,' Houston bitterly told his wife.

War fever again swept Texas. Members of

the cabinet denounced Houston when he refused to call for volunteers. But Houston stood firm in his belief that the skirmishes were only a harassment on the part of Santa Anna.

'There is no money in the treasury to finance a war!' Houston told his cabinet. He then sent a scorching letter to Santa Anna, reminding the Mexican dictator of his treaty obligations.

It was the same old story. *El Presidente* was in trouble with his own people again. They were sick of his tyranny. Santa Anna had decided that pointing the finger at Texas would help salvage his own decadent regime.

Although Houston continued to urge caution, believing Santa Anna would not dare launch a full-scale offensive against Texas, others clamored for action.

He received a letter from Jesse Summer. Summer was about to join the proposed Mier expedition, which Houston was denouncing as foolhardy, an act that would bring the Republic face to face with a war it could ill afford.

'I hope by this action,' Summer wrote, 'to at least partially redeem myself in your eyes.'

★　　　★　　　★

Although Jesse Summer did not know Houston's attitude toward the war that was threatening, his one desire was to try at long last to make something of his life, to do some

195

constructive thing.

Captain William Fisher, who had fought in the service of Mexico before independence, had decided to carry the war to the Mexicans. Jesse Summer, armed with a new rifle and pistol, joined the jubilant band of three hundred.

Across the border they struck suddenly at the town of Mier. So fierce was the Texan attack that Mexican resistance was quickly broken. With the town secure, Captain Fisher came grinning to where Summer stood sentry duty.

'When news of what we've done reaches Texas,' Fisher told him, 'we'll have more volunteers than we can use.'

'It's time we stood up to the Mexicans,' one of the Texans muttered, 'whether Sam Houston likes it or not.'

'Sam knows what he's doing,' Summer said thoughtfully. 'I know him well.'

'Houston will be eager enough to share in our triumphs,' Fisher snapped, and walked away from the bullet-scarred wall where they had been standing.

'We should have waited for word from Houston,' Summer told the man next to him, a bearded Texan named Needham.

'Bah, we need no word from him.'

Summer frowned. He hadn't known until the town was captured that Houston did not favor the venture.

He looked around at the town, where some of

the Texans were celebrating the victory. And he thought of a similar celebration at San Antonio de Bexar when he and Mike Reardon had fought over a harlot.

Again, as he had so many times in the past, he wondered what fate Reardon had suffered in this life.

And as he watched the citizens of this town of Mier, he wondered if the Texans had really committed a blunder by taking this place. The Mexicans were angry, sullen. They hated Santa Anna, but they hated the Texans even more. And now with invasion their resistance would stiffen. Nowhere was there any sound of joy that they had been liberated from Santa Anna's yoke.

Summer knew then that Houston's reluctance to declare war was wise. Because the Mexicans were like a quarreling family. The members might fight among themselves, but when danger threatened from outside the family circle, they drew together.

He stared in the direction of Texas, wondering what Sam Houston might be doing this day. Houston had expected great things from him. *And I*, Summer thought with a bitter smile, *expected greater things from myself.*

Needham shouted, 'Here they come!'

Summer wheeled. Emerging from a cloud of dust was a large force of Mexican soldiers. Over

197

two thousand, he judged, complete with cavalry.

Needham fingered his beard nervously. 'I figure we oughta run for it.'

'We're a little late,' Summer told him grimly.

Already the mounted troops were swinging in a great circle to cut off any escape toward Texas. From the town came the shouts of alerted Texans. A tall man hurried by, a rifle in one hand, a jug wrapped in a crimson petticoat in the other.

'Just when I fix to have myself a time, then we got to fight,' he complained to Summer.

There was a sudden burst of rifle fire from the Mexican ranks. The tall Texan sat down suddenly on the hard ground. The left side of his chest was red.

'You hurt bad?' Summer asked, hurrying up.

'They got me, but they never touched my jug. How about giving me a drink from it?'

Summer reached for the jug wrapped in the petticoat. When he turned to give the wounded man a drink, he saw that the Texan was dead.

Needham, who had come up to stare, said, 'You take a drink, Summer. Then pass that jug to me. I got a burning in my gut. I never seen so damn many Mexicans in my life.'

A drum beat a roll as Summer took his drink. A citizen of Mier came storming from the house where he had barricaded himself against the invading Texans. He carried a rusted old musket which he tried to fire at Needham's back.

'Viva Mexico!' the Mexican shouted.

Summer shot him in the leg and the Mexican dropped the musket and crawled back into the house.

Summer handed the jug to Needham. He stared at the crimson petticoat, wondering if it had been given willingly to the dead Texan or taken by force. Summer let it fall beside the body of the man who had been killed.

'Brings the war close to home,' Summer said, his throat tight from a growing anxiety. 'I've seen death, but never quicker or more complete.'

Needham was wiping whisky from his beard, staring out at the Mexicans, who were making a great clamor. The cavalry stormed one way and another, their horses prancing. A rifle boomed from a rooftop and a horse and rider went down.

'I purely figure we got ourselves in a trap,' Needham said, worried.

'I guess Fisher didn't think there were this many troops within a hundred miles.'

'He should have had scouts out.'

Fisher was waving his sword at them. 'Down here, you two. We'll concentrate our fire. We can stand them off!'

They started down the slant toward a row of houses where the Texans were going to make their fight. On the way Needham stumbled.

The jug smashed against a rock. 'Damn,' he said mournfully, picking himself up: 'Figured we could at least have drunk that dead fella's whisky.'

All that day the Mexicans hurled charge after charge against the town, the deepest penetration being made by the cavalry. Summer, lying flat on the ground, his rifle stock against his cheek, overcame a natural revulsion at the killing of animals. As he had learned years ago, the best way to stop a cavalry charge was by unhorsing the riders.

As the Mexicans came thundering toward their breastworks, Summer sighted on the broad breastbone of a racing gray. Astride the gray was a trooper with a tight-lipped brown face. He was waving a sword and shouting with the others in the long line that came at a hard run.

Jesse Summer squeezed the trigger and the great horse came down, throwing its rider almost at Summer's feet. Dazed, the rider struggled up. A Texan on Summer's right shot the Mexican through the throat.

Under a withering fire, the cavalry fell back.

'We can't keep this up forever,' one of the men said, peering through clouds of powder smoke at the Mexicans.

'I imagine this is how Travis and Bowie felt at the Alamo,' Summer said thinly.

'Let's hope it don't turn out like the Alamo,'

Needham put in. 'Wish I hadn't busted that jug. I could sure stand a drink.'

Again the Mexicans stormed Mier, and again they were driven back. But the Texas ammunition was running low. Captain Fisher gravely urged his men to be sure of their targets.

After eighteen hours of constant pressure, Captain Fisher was forced to capitulate.

Returning from negotiations for surrender, he walked with a Mexican captain. 'Put down your arms, men,' Fisher ordered. For a moment Jesse Summer hesitated. He had a premonition that if he put down his weapons, it would mean the end. He clung to his rifle and pistol.

Fisher gestured angrily. 'That means you, Summer. Put down those weapons. Do you want to get us all shot?'

Reluctantly, Summer did as he was ordered. Glancing to his left, he saw that Needham's beard seemed unusually dark against the pallor of the Texan's face.

No sooner were they disarmed than the terms of surrender were violated.

'You will be paraded before *El Presidente* himself!' boasted the Mexican commander.

He ordered the captured Texans to be tied, two by two. Although Captain Fisher protested this outrage, he was powerless to prevent it. For the next several days the Texans were herded toward Mexico City. At each step their rage increased.

Summer, his right wrist lashed to Needham's left, whispered, 'We'll watch our chance, then make a break for it.'

'I hope to God we get that chance,' Needham breathed. 'I'd rather get shot trying to escape than face what's ahead of us in Mexico City.'

That night they had a meager ration of dried beef and sour beans. Aside from guards spaced some thirty feet apart, the Texans were alone. The main body of Mexican troops was gathered around huge campfires down in a hollow. A guitar strummed and somebody sang of love in old Chihuahua. Horses in a rope corral stirred nervously some distance away.

'If we could only get our hands on those horses,' Summer whispered. But he knew they could never fight their way to the mounts.

Summer noted that the nearest guard wore a heavy knife at his belt. He gestured toward the guard and said in a low voice, 'We'll have to do it together, Needham. Pretend you're sick and follow my lead.'

Needham nodded and they staggered up, Summer with a large rock in his hand. With their wrists lashed together, they moved through the darkness toward the sentry.

As they approached, the sentry snapped to attention. '*Alto!*' he hissed. 'Halt!'

202

Summer pointed at Needham. 'My friend, he is ill. His stomach—'

The sentry looked suspiciously at Needham, who was bent over, his free hand pressed against his midsection.

'No, no,' the sentry grunted, and started to back up so he could level the long-barreled rifle.

Summer lashed out with the stone in his hand. The rock caught the sentry on the joint of the jaw. As he went down soundlessly, Needham snatched his rifle. Sweating, despite the chill and moonless night, Summer drew the sentry's knife. He slashed the bonds that held his wrist to Needham's. Glancing toward the fires, he saw that the Mexican troops were still singing, laughing, evidently in high spirits. The other sentries apparently had not noticed anything wrong.

With the knife Summer freed as many of the Texas prisoners as he could. Then as moonlight started to color the eastern sky, they hurried away on foot, screened by brush, hoping to cover as many miles as possible before daybreak.

They ran, walked, trotted, then ran again. Finally exhaustion claimed them and they drew up in a fold of the hills to rest. At dawn they were up again, traveling at the same shambling gait. Suddenly they heard horses and saw the Mexican cavalry bearing down on them.

Needham had the only weapon, the rifle

taken from the fallen sentry. He fired into the troopers, killing a horse.

Screaming their rage, the Mexican cavalry bore down on Needham, who had started to flee. Their sword literally cut him to pieces.

Sickened at the sight, Summer was herded with the others past the mutilated body of Needham. Hours later, staggering now, completely spent, they reached the main camp they had left last night.

The other prisoners greeted them solemnly. 'Sorry you didn't make it boys,' one of them said.

The Mexican commander said, 'I will be satisfied with *diezmo*—one in ten. To pay for this outrage, I will execute one man in ten.'

The Texans received this news in stunned silence, and no amount of protest would alter the commander's decision.

There were 176 prisoners. Summer felt himself dying slowly inside as he saw some of the *soldados* count out 159 white beans and 17 black ones. These were put in a pot. Then the prisoners lined up.

When it came Summer's turn to plunge his hand into the pot, he closed his eyes. Withdrawing his hand, he looked at the bean he had picked. It was black.

He was ordered to stand aside with the others who had been marked for death. Those already in the group tried to joke about it.

'Welcome, Summer,' one of them said. 'Looks like we're something special.'

'Wish I could spit in Santa Anna's eye,' another said, 'before they kill me.'

Summer said, 'I didn't quite plan on dying this way.'

One of the younger Texans said to the captain in charge of the execution party, 'Will you put a cross on my grave?'

The young captain, who showed no pleasure over his assignment, did not reply. They were marched to a dirt bank and there lined up. Far down the hollow the rest of the prisoners looked on silently. Some of them lifted hands in farewell.

'You wish the eyes covered, *Señores?*' the captain asked solicitously.

'The hell with you!' somebody said.

Summer got a tight smile on his face as the double file of Mexican troops formed across the clearing.

'*Adios*, Sam,' Summer said, staring over the heads of the firing squad. 'I wish I'd taken your advice. Maybe now I could be helping you run that government of yours.'

Rifle fire smashed across the clearing. Summer felt the fierce shock of the bullet. In him was a sort of bubbling effervescence instead of pain. Helplessly he watched as the tilted earth crashed into his face...

CHAPTER SIXTEEN

In 1844, with the election of Polk as President of the United States annexation became a political issue once again. This time the move was successful. However, it impelled Mexico to declare war. But Houston, elected United States Senator with Thomas J. Ruck, was in Washington, fighting for Texas, no longer a republic, but now a state.

During the years that followed talk of secession inflamed the Southern bloc. Although a Southerner, Houston agitated against it, and in time he stood virtually alone, hated by his own people. Yet neither would he cater to the Northern Abolitionists, whom he termed eager to free the black man, but having no interest in the impoverished condition of the redman.

At the start of the presidential campaign of 1856 there was a small boom launched among Northern Democrats to draft Houston for the office. But he made no attempt to further his own candidacy.

'I'm sixty-five years old,' he told Margaret. 'I am tiring of public life. I will make no effort to seek re-election. I want my home and my family and nothing more.'

On February 26, 1859, he delivered his farewell speech to the Senate, ending it with a prayer for the continuation of the Union.

However, the private life he had longed for was far from satisfying and he ran for governor against Runnels. Although there was much opposition to him because of his anti-secesh view, he beat Runnels.

And the people said, 'We voted not for his ideas, but because he is "Old Sam."'

In his inaugural address he stated: 'Texas will maintain the situation and stand by the Union. It is all that can save us as a nation. Destroy it and anarchy awaits us.'

Because rabid states-righters were openly proclaiming that if 'black Lincoln' was elected President it was a call for secession, Houston rose from a sickbed to address a mass-meeting at Austin.

'The Union,' he urged, 'is worth more than Mr. Lincoln, and if the battle is to be fought for the constitution, let us fight it in the Union for the sake of the Union.'

But Houston's plea fell upon deaf ears. Of the 80,000 voters in Texas, nearly half stayed away from the polls, with the result that 34,415 voted for secession and 13,841 against it.

Heart-broken because again the people of Texas had ignored his advice, Houston sat in his office while a convention elected delegates to the Confederate Congress in Montgomery. When this was done Houston's enemies made a surprise move to drive him from office.

On March 14 an ordinance was adopted requiring all state officers to take an oath of allegiance to the Confederacy.

'This I will never do!' Houston cried.

In a final address as governor, Houston said: 'I love Texas too well to bring civil strife and bloodshed upon her. To avert this calamity I shall make no endeavor to maintain my authority as chief executive of the state, except by peaceful exercise of my functions. When I can no longer do this, I shall calmly withdraw from the scene.'

When he declined to take the oath of allegiance to the Confederacy, an official order declared the office of governor to be vacant.

Even though he was no longer in political power, Houston continued to warn the citizens of the black years that would result from Texas' withdrawal from the Union.

Everywhere he was condemned as a traitor. But when his son, Young Sam, wanted to enlist in the Confederate Army, he offered no objections.

Houston visited his son in training at Galveston and when asked by the colonel to review the regiment, did so, wearing his old uniform from San Jacinto days.

Tiredly he sat his horse and watched the ranks of gray-clad troops march smartly by. How many would die, he thought bitterly, in the years ahead.

A great depression gripped him as the North and South were locked in battle. Even though the Confederacy seemed victorious in early engagements, he knew the war's outcome would find the South and his beloved Texas beaten to her knees.

'The Union has superiority in manpower and money,' Houston told Margaret.

'If only they had listened to you,' she said and put a handkerchief to her eyes.

Exhaustion induced by anxiety over the war brought him to the edge of the grave in 1862. But he still refused to die. In March, 1863, the people of Houston, fearful of the future, looked upon him once again as the leader who could bring them comfort in the dark days.

They begged Old Sam for a speech.

Disregarding doctors' orders, he addressed a large crowd, saying in part, 'Ere I step forward to journey through the pilgrimage of death, I would say that all my thoughts and all my hopes are with my country. If one impulse arises before another, it is for the happiness of these people; the welfare and glory of Texas will be uppermost while the spark of life lingers in this breast.'

His days were numbered now and though he occasionally took short walks in the sun, leaning on his cane, he found his horizons growing dim. Though Margaret stayed close to him, a sense of loneliness and sadness gripped him. He knew the South was doomed and the thought of all the suffering and dying on both sides was a heavy weight deep inside him.

It was news of the fall of Vicksburg that shocked him so severely that he took to his bed.

'All hope is gone now,' he told Margaret. 'So much death, so needlessly.'

Three weeks later, on July 26, 1863, he died in the arms of his wife, his last words being, 'Texas—Texas—'